THE
AMPLIFIER PROTOCOL

Library and Archives Canada
Doidge, Meghan Ciana, 1973—
The Amplifier Protocol/Meghan Ciana Doidge—
PAPERBACK

Cover design by Gene Mollica
Model: Devon Ericksen
Oracle Cards designed by Elizabeth Mackey

ISBN 978-1-927850-94-7

THE
AMPLIFIER
PROTOCOL

MEGHAN CIANA DOIDGE

Published by Old Man in the CrossWalk Productions
Salt Spring Island, BC, Canada

www.madebymeghan.ca

The Adept Universe is comprised of the Dowser, the Oracle, the Reconstructionist, and the Amplifier series. While it is not necessary to read all three series, **in order to avoid spoilers** the ideal reading order of the Adept Universe is as follows:

Other books in the Amplifier series to follow.

More information can be found at
www.madebymeghan.ca/novels

For Michael
Tattooed. On my heart.

THE AMPLIFIER PROTOCOL

THE AMPLIFIER SERIES: BOOK 0

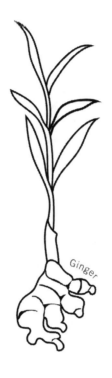

Ginger

MANIFESTATION

AUTHOR'S NOTE

The Amplifier Protocol is the prequel novella for the Amplifier series, which is set in the same universe as the Dowser, Oracle, and Reconstructionist series.

The Amplifier Protocol (Amplifier 0)
Close to Home (Amplifier 0.5)
Demons and DNA (Amplifier 1)

THEY CALLED ME AN AMPLIFIER. AND THEY HAD bred me, raised me, and trained me to be a killer with preternatural precision. I was capable of taking, holding, and transferring power that wasn't my own with a simple touch. Skin-to-skin contact. Along with four others of my generation, I could infiltrate any magical organization, extracting whoever or whatever I'd been ordered to extricate. Then I could destroy all evidence of our passing presence.

They had made me. They directed me. Controlled me.

Then they tried to kill me.

ONE

MARCH 2011.

I exited the building onto the roof thirteen minutes after I'd entered via the ground floor. In that time, I had disabled all magical and mundane security, eliminated any resistance, and retrieved the package on the fifteenth floor. Now I was arriving at the extraction point, two minutes ahead of schedule.

A transport helicopter blew past, circling the building. The sound of its blades was magically dampened, but the obfuscation spell coating its black hull was doing a terrible job of obscuring it from sight. And it wasn't going to hold in broad daylight for much longer.

Nul5 and Tek5 darted ahead. The nullifier and telekinetic systematically swept the rooftop, visually checking that the area was clear of adversaries. I could sense that it was, but relying solely on magical senses was negligent. And we were anything but inept. The black armor they wore was stark against the landscape of pale gray, blue, and white buildings that occupied the downtown core of Los Angeles. It was the same armor I wore, magically fortified and flexible, but neither of them carried the twin blades sheathed between my shoulder blades.

The sky was hazy, the temperature typical for early spring. At least that was what had been highlighted as need-to-know on the mission brief. Some spells were affected by extreme changes in temperature or an excessive amount of sunlight.

Bristling with magic, the remainder of the extraction team flanked me, ready to protect the package at all costs. After more than two years together, we had little or no need for comms, magical or mundane. We would often move in silence, instinctively working together without the need for verbal orders. When orders were necessary, I had the final say. But I usually deferred to the commanding officer, Mark Calhoun.

We cleared the egress, hunkering down to the side of the upper stairwell to wait for a direct path to the pickup.

Jackson peeled away from the group, stepping back to the steel exterior door. She pulled a roll of red tape from the zippered pocket on her upper left thigh. Starting at the bottom right corner, she ran the tape up and then across the edges of the door, revealing a series of inked runes. Adhering the tape to the steel and concrete, she activated a barrier spell with a bluntly uttered command.

Energy flashed through the inked runes, sealing the door behind us. Sorcerer magic. Becca Jackson, aka X3, was the team's demolitions expert, but her magic worked both ways—securing or shattering as needed.

Sunlight cut through the permanent haze that hung over the city, momentarily blinding me as it reflected off something to the west. I angled my head, clearing my sight line but sensing nothing magically amiss. Though securing the extraction point wasn't my task. It was exceedingly unlikely that an adversary could have gotten any threat—magical or otherwise—past Cla5 or Tel5. And the clairvoyant and the telepath were monitoring the mission from the roof of a neighboring building.

The helicopter circled to set down. I reached back for the package, ready to run with him. He'd been tortured by magical means, but had made it most of the way up the stairs on his own two feet, supported between Piper and Hannigan. As a werewolf, Sasha Piper, aka X5, was the enforcer for the team—stronger, faster, and more brutal than everyone but me. The sorcerer Tom Hannigan, aka X4, was a shield specialist.

The team huddling around me were all weapon wielders, but I preferred to keep my hands free. I was more effective in close contact situations. So in corridors and stairwells, I'd lead with Nul5, who would nullify any offensive spells. But in an open area, such as the rooftop, the team would take the lead.

The package shifted closer to me. Cool fingers sought out and found the naked skin between my glove and sleeve, wrapping around my wrist. I glanced down. His own skin was medium brown, fingernails manicured into a smooth shine. A prickle of energy shifted between us—my empathy power, bringing his heightened emotions with it. I felt his lingering fear, coupled with relief. Pain and weariness. He'd been lashed to a chair, barely conscious when I'd found him.

I had drained two of his shapeshifter captors myself, taking the first before the other had even known I was in the room. The second fell while she was still staring at her partner in morbid terror as I'd incapacitated him. Or perhaps it had been specifically me who'd terrified her. Which was ironic, since she was the one who could transform into a six-and-a-half-foot-tall, razor-clawed, half-human / half-beast warrior form capable of rending someone limb from limb with minimal exertion.

In an effort to revive the sorcerer I'd been tasked to rescue, I had channeled the stolen energy from the shapeshifters into him. It wasn't possible for a nonshifter to transform, of course. That ability was rooted in shifter DNA, in their blood. But the stolen energy was enough to get the package on his feet.

A fierce satisfaction flooded through me. It wasn't my own emotion, though.

It was the sorcerer's.

Touching me had been deliberate. And risky, since he'd witnessed what I could do with skin-to-skin contact. Twice.

My latent empathy picked up a smugness in his satisfaction. A possessiveness.

He knew me.

I met his dark eyed gaze. The wind picked up from the helicopter landing on the roof, lifting the sorcerer's dark-brown hair from his high forehead. It was silvered at the temples. Strong, straight nose. Narrow chin. The fine lines around his dark, defiant eyes had been exacerbated by dehydration and sleep deprivation.

I didn't recognize him.

He twisted his lips into a proud sneer. His accent was lilting and precise. "You are as magnificent as I always intended you to be, amplifier."

Shock slammed through me. My own emotion this time, triggered by a burst of adrenaline. I twisted my wrist in his grasp, breaking his hold. Even if he hadn't been magically drained, he couldn't have held me. Not with physical force.

Few people could hold me, even with my magic at normal levels. And despite what I'd shared with the sorcerer, the act of draining two shapeshifters of their magic had let me momentarily harness their innate strength on top of my own permanently stolen power. Power that amplifiers didn't simply inherit. At least not other amplifiers, even as rare as they might be among those who possessed magic. The Adept.

I wasn't just an amplifier, though. I'd been genetically constructed. I was the result of over a century of magical and scientific experiments. And over the past twenty-one years, I'd been forced to siphon magic from others. Forced to claim strength, heightened healing, and other abilities for my own—and often killing those I plundered in the process.

The empathy I'd inadvertently stolen from my birth mother—my first victim—never allowed me to become fully numb to the process.

I focused on the present situation. The sorcerer knew me.

He claimed responsibility for me.

So he was one of the Collective.

I'd been sent to rescue a nameless asset, though obviously one of high value. And I had wound up retrieving one of the architects of my conception—the Collective who had begot the Five.

A chill ran down my spine that had nothing to do with the warmth of the day, and everything to do with the disconcertion of meeting—

Incoming! Tel5 screamed through the telepathic connection that bound the core team together.

A deafening roar accompanied by a bright wash of light—some sort of magical, mental backlash—assaulted all my senses, sending me face first toward the concrete roof. Tel5's near-constant presence in my mind was wiped away, leaving me mentally shaken in a way I'd never felt before.

"Calhoun!" I barked. I managed to hold myself upright, but just barely. "Do you have comms?"

Mark Calhoun, situated to my left and slightly ahead, flicked his hazel eyes my way briefly, shaking his head sharply. The commanding officer's automatic weapon remained raised and ready, scanning the rooftop. "We've been cut off," he said, referring to the electronic comms he and most other members of the team carried. None of them were mentally linked and bound to the telepath as Nul5, Tek5, and I were through our blood tattoos.

Like the weapons the others carried, Calhoun's was modified to shoot magically imbued silver rounds. The extraction team had been well briefed about what and who we'd be facing. We had armed ourselves accordingly. Unfortunately, there was a new adversary on the field. An Adept who was capable of knocking out magical and electronic communication with equal ease. Or perhaps more than one Adept.

The exterior door blew open, taking Jackson with it and nearly decapitating the members of the extraction team on my right.

Shapeshifters in warrior form swarmed the roof. Six-and-a-half-foot-tall half-human / half-beasts with three-inch-long claws and deadly sharp teeth. Physically stronger and faster than over two-thirds of my team, and with an innate resistance to magical assault. Thankfully, the specialty rounds we were carrying would even the odds.

Flynn and Hannigan raised their weapons, taking the first three shifters down with headshots.

I grabbed the package, heaving him across my shoulders, and ran toward the helicopter. Leaving

Jackson to fend for herself, the core of the extraction team moved with me, systematically taking down any targets that attempted to impede our progress.

Sasha Piper was ripped away into a swarm of claws and teeth on my right. Even magically muffled, the gunfire was compromising my hearing. But I didn't need to be able to hear to reach my objective.

As I moved, I felt the magic of the sorcerer across my back collecting, coalescing as he readied some massive spell with the last vestiges of his power.

Tek5 stood with her back to the open side of the helicopter, its rotor blades whirling overhead. She flung her hands out, stretching toward a rooftop ventilation unit to my left. Her dark-brown skin glistened, glints of her telekinesis seen in the sheen of sweat that slicked her face from having stood in the sun for too long.

Nul5 was down, sprawled at the telekinetic's feet, but shaking his head. The psychic blast had apparently hit the nullifier much harder than it had me or Tek5.

That was unexpected.

The ventilation unit ripped free from its bolted base, metal twisting, denting. With a flick of her hands, Tek5 launched the unit across my path, slamming it into and clearing any combatants that had gotten ahead of my charge.

With the first wave knocked off the field, the shapeshifters tearing at the edges of the extraction team changed tactics. Moving as if they were also telepathically linked, they swarmed to intercept Tek5 and the helicopter. They instinctively perceived her to be the biggest threat.

And they weren't wrong.

They were simply ignorant, placing themselves between me and my goal. It was always foolish to get between me and an objective.

I ripped my left glove off with my teeth, reaching over my shoulder to press my hand to the sorcerer's face. He wrapped both of his hands around mine, giving me permission just by touching me.

Just by knowing what I could do.

That thought, that development, would have to wait to be explored until I had the package safely on the helicopter and my team back at base.

Flynn fell, leaving an opening at my left flank that Calhoun immediately filled. The commanding officer's shift of position opened me up to a frontal attack. But whatever I faced directly would always go down, so guarding my rear was the priority.

I took the sorcerer's magic. I took the spell he murmured against my ear. I harnessed the power he'd called forth, conducting it as it willed. I thrust my free hand forward. A spiral of darkly tinted energy flowed down my arm.

"Your left!" I screamed. Then I pumped my own power into the sorcerer's casting to double it … to triple it in strength.

Ahead, Tek5 and Nul5 dropped to the concrete, each rolling to their left.

I released the spell. A spell I had no actual ability to call, command, or control. Dark energy streamed from my splayed fingers, hitting the five nearest shapeshifters. They dropped, writhing and howling in pain.

Calhoun and Hannigan eliminated the last two shifters between the helicopter and our charge. But there were still a half-dozen or more behind us. Shifter magic was difficult to distinguish when they were grouped together, and I couldn't take my focus off my objective to glance back.

Nul5 darted around the helicopter, wrenching open the pilot's door and yanking him out of his seat. A prudent decision. We'd been telepathically cut off from Tel5 and Cla5, as well as from the comms. That was a feat I would have declared impossible—if I ever entertained the notion of impossibilities. Which I didn't.

There was no way of knowing who was loyal, except for the Five. And two of us were already un-accounted for. Not knowing what had happened to Cla5 and Tel5 meant that everything and everyone but the package was expendable.

But that had always been the case.

It would always be the case.

The Five were an arm, a weapon, of the Collect-ive. We went where we were ordered, did what we were told to do. And the team of specialists backing us was even more expendable than we were.

The pilot rolled to his feet, palming a weapon and firing at the nearest shifter as he ran toward us.

Also a prudent move. Even if he wasn't a regular team member, there was strength in numbers. And the extraction team was the second-largest grouping on the roof.

Tek5 appeared out of nowhere, perched suddenly on the edge of the helicopter's side door. She had triggered her short-range teleportation ability to move into place swiftly. She kept her gaze glued to me, ready to grab the package.

The space between us was clear of adversaries.

To my immediate right and without any warning, Hannigan turned his automatic weapon on me.

Tom Hannigan. Shield specialist. He'd been with us for two years.

Unfortunately for him, he wasn't fast enough to both aim and pull the trigger. Not even at point-blank range.

Still running, still carrying the sorcerer, I grabbed the weapon, smashing it back into Hannigan's face and dropping him. The harsh double bark of a weapon behind me informed me that Calhoun had finished off the would-be traitor without even pausing.

Steps away from Tek5, I shifted the sorcerer from across my shoulders. The telekinetic grabbed his arm, hauling him up into the helicopter.

I followed, getting the sorcerer settled in a seat and belting him in as quickly as I could without hurting him.

Calhoun and the pilot stayed on the roof, guarding our backs.

"Took you long enough, Socks," Nul5 shouted from the pilot's seat. His hands were flying over the controls, double-checking everything. A sensible precaution, since some sort of betrayal was apparently in the process of unfolding.

Tek5 laughed wickedly, flush with energy and magic as she tugged on a headset.

I ignored them both.

The sorcerer's fingers ghosted my cheek.

I met his dark-eyed gaze.

Tek5 caught the exchange. A deep frown instantly replaced her former playfulness.

The sorcerer held a headset in his other hand, having already put on another pair. I took it from him and put it on.

"Socks?" The sorcerer's tone was weary but amused, even through the headset speakers. He touched my face again. "Is that your name, amplifier? I'm Kader Azar. I would have you know me."

"I have no name, Sorcerer Azar. I am simply a designation. Amp5. As you well know."

He dropped his hand, but not before I'd felt a spark of his anger.

Calhoun shouted something outside the copter, but his words were obscured by the headset and the steady thump of the blades overhead. I twisted around to take in the scene on the roof.

The shapeshifters had fallen back, carrying their wounded and swarming the exit.

It wasn't a strategic retreat.

A dark-scaled, double-horned, red-eyed demon was in the process of clawing its way over the edge of the roof. I had never seen such a massive creature before, not called forth from our or any other dimension. And the Five had confronted many demons, both in training and on mission. Just its head, neck, and shoulders were the size of a compact car.

Keeping my gaze on the demon, I double-checked the harness holding the sorcerer, Azar, in his seat. Then I sought out and quickly located the fallen members of my team. One was sprawled out in the open, dead—Hannigan, X4. One was running for the helicopter, exposed—Flynn, X2. Jackson, X3, had managed to make it across the roof on her own, and was now grouped with Calhoun and the pilot.

One of them was hunkered down behind the twisted ventilation unit that Tek5 had tossed across the roof, vulnerable. Sasha Piper, X5.

I yanked off the headset, moving for the side door.

Tek5 grabbed my arm, screaming, "We're going!"

"Yes," I said. "You are."

"You're coming with us! The package is all that matters."

"Find out what's going on with Cla5 and Tel5, would you?" I didn't like being cut off from the telepath and clairvoyant. Something had happened—something severe enough that Tel5 hadn't reestablished contact yet. And the telepath had been backed by a clairvoyant, who should have seen whatever hit them at least a few moments before it actually happened.

But I had to focus on the situation immediately in front of me first. My extraction team couldn't stand against what I was assuming was some sort of greater demon. Though using that Christian classification as a reference wasn't terribly accurate, it was a convenient shortcut. Demons were pulled or summoned into the earth's dimension. They didn't come from hell, at least according to the years of study we had all dedicated to them. The Collective limited our access to information in many ways, though, so what I knew about demons might have been only what they wanted me to know.

But one of the facts that had always been made clear to me was that I'd been created and honed—even separate from the Five—to stand against the kind of creature making its way onto the roof.

Disbelief flitted over Tek5's face. She tightened her grip on me, snarling over her shoulder to Nul5 in the pilot's seat. "Go! Go!"

The helicopter lifted. I twisted my arm from Tek5's firm grasp, jumping for the open door.

"Socks!" Nul5 shouted behind me.

I dropped to the roof, rolling to quickly gain my feet. Calhoun, Flynn, Jackson, and the pilot instantly flanked me. A raw wound was slashed across Jackson's forehead and cheek, likely from the breaching of the exterior door. Flynn's right arm was hanging limp. But their magical armor had taken the brunt of the shapeshifters' assault. Calhoun and the pilot appeared unharmed.

Across the roof, Sasha Piper had extracted herself from the shapeshifters but was now trapped behind the huge vent that Tek5 had flung across the roof. The demon was between her and the exit.

Three sorcerers, including two weapons specialists and a demolitions expert. The pilot, who was a witch by the tenor of his magic, but likely also a technician. Plus me. And not one of us was prepped to face a demon like the creature that had just found its footing and was straightening up to a full height of easily six meters.

Behind us, the helicopter began to circle overhead. I ignored it, but it drew the demon's attention.

Following my lead without any need for direction, what was left of my team darted forward with me. I paused by X4, kneeling beside him. He was dead. Two efficient shots to the side of his head. I took his gun and extra ammo, glancing over at Calhoun for the briefest of moments.

Hannigan's betrayal was unexpected. Unprecedented. So who else had he been working for? I might not have been able to pick up emotions without direct skin contact, but Tel5 should have been able to root out even a hint of betrayal with a stray thought.

I passed my hands over the body, quickly emptying its multitude of pockets. I collected a pile of spelled coins and rune-marked stones, passing them to the others to distribute between them. Then I found what I was looking for.

A gold-plated magical artifact. Something that appeared to have once been a brooch. The pin had been removed and a compartment added to the back. I clicked it open, dispelling a sealing spell without effort. The tiny clipping of yellow hair housed within the compartment blew away as the helicopter circled a second time.

Tel5 had yellow hair. Though not much of it. All of the Five were ordered to keep our hair short enough to stay out of our eyes.

A clipping of hair.

Yet another impossibility.

The betrayal ran deeper than Tom Hannigan, then.

Calhoun hissed something over my head. I didn't catch his words but his pissed tone was obvious, indicating that he'd put together the depth of the disloyalty himself.

I tucked the brooch into my pocket, adding it to the to-do list for after I got what remained of my team off the roof and back to base. I straightened, first checking, then raising and firmly pressing X4's purloined automatic weapon into my shoulder. I was a fair shot, but it wasn't in any way a talent. Unfortunately, simply touching the demon wasn't going to be an effective way to take the creature down. Its magic was incompatible with my own. Incompatible with anything in this dimension.

The magic of whoever had summoned the demon could be thwarted, though. It could be nullified. Unfortunately, the two best means to uncover that summoner's location were currently out of contact—Cla5 and Tel5. Nul5 would have been a third option, but he was piloting the helicopter, distracting the dimensional interloper tearing up the concrete of the roof with its massively clawed hind feet. That put him nowhere near enough to nullify any magic that might have been tethering the creature.

Figuring out what a greater demon was doing on a rooftop in LA in broad daylight wasn't a mystery I was going to be able to solve. Primarily because it wasn't my job to figure such things out. I was an infiltration and extraction specialist. A soldier in a private magical army. I was given objectives. I didn't solve puzzles. And asking questions wasn't encouraged by the Collective.

I had already achieved my primary objective, getting the package onto the helicopter. But the demon, and possibly the summoner, had become another obstacle to overcome in order to fully complete the mission.

First, though, I had the rest of my team to collect.

I darted sharply left, crossing directly in front of the demon toward Sasha Piper. The team moved with me.

I couldn't see any shapeshifters, and they appeared to have taken their fallen as they'd exited the roof. Their loyalty was ensured through pack bonds that gave them an advantage against almost any invading force. Except for the Five.

The Five had been uniquely bred and trained from infancy to overcome anything we faced. Together. But if all else failed, the Collective could and would place me alone against any being, any organization, that threatened them. I was their ultimate weapon. In theory.

Even after twenty-one years, that was all I'd figured out regarding my existence. My purpose. But none of it was pertinent to the current situation.

The helicopter circled a third time, completely breaking protocol. Neither Tek5 nor Nul5 could cast any magic while surrounded by electronics, but their tactic of buzzing the roof was annoying the demon and buying me time.

I hunkered down behind the vent beside Piper, stripping off my remaining glove while eyeing the helicopter.

Azar was standing at the open side door, gazing down at the roof. Watching me, not the demon. Tek5 had allowed the sorcerer to unbelt himself, even as drained as he was after I'd channeled the last licks of his magic. That was ill advised. Though I could understand why the telekinetic would have caved if Azar had started throwing his weight around. None of the Five could say no to a member of the Collective. No matter the demand. Not without repercussions.

"Report," Calhoun barked.

"Broken leg," Sasha Piper said. "Ribs possibly fractured. Healing. Slowly."

I offered her my hands, palms up. She met my gaze grimly. Then she nodded, grasping onto me. I blasted her with my amplification. I didn't have time to be gentle.

The green of Sasha's shapeshifter magic flooded her eyes. She grunted, clenching her jaw and straining her neck to suppress a howl of pain. Amplifying someone wasn't usually a painful process. But forcing someone's magic to heal them quickly? That hurt.

And my empathy ensured that I felt the reflection of that pain. I could dampen that sense, though I couldn't suppress it completely. And I could do so even less effectively while using my primary power.

Sasha's hands went limp in mine. She slumped sideways. I let her go, glancing at the others. "She'll need a minute."

They nodded. That wasn't news to them. Each of them had been subjected to my not-so-gentle touch at some point in the time we had worked together.

Screams drew our attention back to the demon. It had caught a shapeshifter that must have been in hiding, and was currently in the process of playing with him. Or her. I couldn't distinguish gender from this far away.

"Jesus," Becca Jackson muttered. "I thought they'd all gotten off the roof."

Sasha woke with a jerk. For a moment, her face rippled as her wolf—amplified by me—tried to tear through her skin. She got herself under control with a gasp, though she pinned me with her blazing green eyes.

With the exception of power I'd just boosted, I didn't normally see magic in color.

"We need to move," Calhoun barked. "While the copter distracts the demon, we make for the exit." He glanced over at the pilot. "Sorry, I don't know your name."

"Sherwood, sir. Bill Sherwood."

"Sherwood, your armor isn't up for this fight. Hang back. If you can break for the exit, you do so." Calhoun glanced at the rest of us in turn. "X5 front, Amp5 between me and X3. X2, you take rear."

The others nodded in unison. Sasha made it to her feet. She and Flynn reorganized and exchanged ammo, guns, and the spells I'd taken off X4, sharing resources. Flynn was moving his arm again, stiffly.

"No," I said.

"No?" Calhoun echoed, completely thrown.

"We can't leave a demon to rampage through LA."

"Not our problem, Amp5."

I didn't bother debating with him. Staying low, I shifted to the side of the ruined ventilation unit so I could get eyes on the demon. Quickly analyzing the way it moved, the way it perceived its surroundings.

Looking for vulnerabilities.

Finding none.

Calhoun was watching me. He was tense, getting angry. I didn't need to touch him to understand what he was feeling. And I was on unstable ground myself. I should have been on the helicopter. I should have been overseeing the process of dropping the package at the rendezvous point, then heading back to base. I should have placed those other objectives over my team.

Instead, I was about to take on a greater demon to get the people who'd fought at my side for years off the roof as safely as possible. The witch psychologist on the Collective's payroll, a low-level empath herself, would no doubt blame my empathic abilities in her report.

Assuming I made it off the roof alive.

"If I fall, reconnoiter at Tel5 and Cla5's last known position." I passed the weapon and ammo I'd taken from Hannigan's corpse to the pilot, Sherwood. He took it without comment. Jackson stepped closer, murmuring a quick orientation of the weapon to the pilot. The wound across her face had crusted over.

Now that I'd gotten a closer look at the immense creature on the roof, as well as the way the dark energy that coated its black-scaled hide reflected the sunlight, I knew the automatic weapon in my hands was useless. It might even backfire on me. "Calhoun," I said. "Judging by the feedback that took me and Nul5 down, I assume Cla5 and Tel5 have been compromised as well. I want you to track them down, eliminate any threats. Then return to base."

"They're not our concern," Calhoun said caustically. "You are. You're the asset here."

I reached over my head, straightening from my low crouch as I pulled my double-edged blades from the sheaths built into my flexible armor between my shoulder blades. Each sword was eighteen inches of steel with a nonreflective black coating, twenty-five inches overall length. Just the right size and weight for simultaneous wielding—assuming you had trained your whole life to fight with twin blades. As I had.

The magic stored in the three raw diamonds embedded in each hilt ignited at my touch, instantly tying the weapons to me, to my magic. They were an extension of my arms now, sharpened by my own power. At least until I wore through the spells, used them up.

Calhoun, Flynn, and Jackson flanked me. Sasha Piper was behind us, with Sherwood hanging farther back. The commanding officer would back me and follow my orders, even if he disagreed.

We crossed from our hiding spot, darting to the center of the roof, giving us the largest cleared area to work within.

The demon homed in on us, spinning back from the edge of the roof and stretching to its full height. It pinned its blazing red eyes on me, as if I had its summoner's sigil tattooed on my forehead.

The helicopter circled once more. I raised my blade, pointing it to my far right, directing it away. It swerved in response. I could practically hear the argument taking place between Nul5 and Tek5, even though I suspected it was the sorcerer Azar who'd kept them on site. Watching me and my team. Nul5 and Tek5 would have stuck to protocol.

If I hadn't actually been carrying him, feeling his magic, I might have concluded that Azar had summoned the demon himself. As some sort of test.

Testing me.

I didn't like having such ideas. I didn't like pontificating on the motivations of those who directed every last thing I did. Everything I ate. Everything I wore. Everyone I killed.

Exacerbating that strange uncertainty was the odd and unsettling feeling of not being mind-connected to the other four. Empty in my head while on the field. But I was trained to act solo. With or without my team.

The demon hunkered down, taking the team in—and once more eyeing me specifically. It was easily still four meters tall on all fours. Its skin was thickly scaled, with spurs of bone jutting up along its spine. Its tail almost doubled its body length, tapering to a single thick spike. It flexed the twelve-inch claws of its front feet, three claws per hand. Curling each individual talon as if anticipating striking at us.

As if it was not only sentient, but capable of acting of its own volition.

Except demons were always following orders. Just like me. Tied to this dimension, tied to their summoners, usually through an object of power. Called forth to wreak bloody havoc by their handlers.

Just like me.

Setting up the summoning of such a creature would have taken days of preparation. And a blood sacrifice. Possibly a human sacrifice. A greater demon didn't simply wander into our dimension uninvited. Doorways had to be opened—usually with dire consequences.

And demons didn't like being controlled. They consumed their summoners the second their hold slipped.

By the way the shapeshifters had fled, they weren't the ones controlling the demon on the roof. And now that I was thinking about it, thinking everything through in order to determine my next move, what did a group of rogue shifters want with a member of the Collective in the first place? How would they even get their claws on a sorcerer of power?

"Form a net," Calhoun barked. "We'll take its legs—"

"No," I said. "The demon is mine. Think it through. Look at the magic coating it. How is it standing in the sun?"

"Shielded," Flynn said.

Piper lifted her face, sniffing the air. "Black magic. Witch."

"I don't give a shit who the summoner is," Calhoun snarled. His magic was coiled tightly around him. Magic that made him the most accurate shot in the group. Magic that eliminated most of the backfires that usually occurred when those of the magical persuasion attempted to use mundane weapons against their own kind. "We're not retreating without you."

I shouldn't have slept with Calhoun the previous night. I shouldn't have wordlessly crawled into his bed. But away from the compound, I'd felt…buoyant. Up to that point, I'd never had sex with anyone but Nul5, who could obviously nullify my magic. Touching Mark Calhoun didn't dampen me, though.

He didn't smother my other senses. And he certainly hadn't minded getting a power boost before a mission.

I had wanted something just for me, just for a moment. Something separate from the Five that I could hold, that I could have for myself.

A choice. A choice made without it being backed by orders or preceded by committee discussion.

For a long while now, every now and then, Mark had looked at me. Across a shared meal or during a recon session. He just looked at me. And in that look, I thought … I felt beautiful, wanted.

He was looking at me that way now, surrounded by team members who deserved our best efforts. Who needed to trust that we would all put our lives on the line for each other. Otherwise, we would cease to function as a unit. And we would all die.

I focused again. I shook my head bluntly. "You are retreating without me. Protocol dictates that the wounded are—"

Calhoun cut me off, switching out his gun for a series of rune-marked stones and a simple slingshot. "You've already seen to that, Amp5. I'm commanding officer of this unit. My orders stand."

Flynn and Jackson separated, facing each other as they dropped their guns across their backs. Each of them snapped their arms up before them, bent at the elbow, readying a dual cast.

"The five of us are more than enough to take down this shit-beast." Sasha Piper let out a rippling snarl behind me. Then her human visage shifted as her own beast tore through her skin to tower over me, all furred muscle, sharp teeth, and rending claws. Her armor was flexible enough to transition with her.

I clenched my teeth, putting my head down and my blades up. I would let the others do their jobs. Arguing any further was a waste of time. Despite the magical protections and the shielding we all wore during a mission—and even hazarding a guess that the magic coating the demon must have been masking it from general view—any minute now, we were going to pull unwanted attention.

As cloistered as I was kept by the Collective, even I knew that beings of power patrolled this world, enforcing rules of magical conduct. The guardians of the magically Adept. If there hadn't been such power, there wouldn't have been any reason for the Collective to form, to unite across magical species, to create the Five. A tool capable of doing all the deeds that would be frowned upon by those who had the power to enforce a basic set of rules on the Adept world.

Such as summoning a greater demon in the middle of LA in broad daylight.

I had a more personal reason for never wanting to meet such a guardian, though. I really didn't want to face anyone or any force that the Collective feared enough that it inspired them to create me. To create the possibility of what I could do.

So. The demon needed to be vanquished, quickly and efficiently. Before it drew any attention.

Flynn and Jackson snapped their magical net into place. Thick ropes of writhing, dark-blue energy stretched between them. Flanked by Calhoun and Piper in her half-beast form, they rushed the demon. I kept pace a few steps behind them. Sherwood stayed behind me.

In practice, the net would take out the demon's back legs, forcing it into a lowered position so that I could finish it off. United, the Five wouldn't have needed the backup of the team or the net at all. But reality rarely unfolded in any way that could be trained for or anticipated.

The demon watched us.

If I hadn't known any better, I would have sworn it looked amused by our antics.

That angered me.

Yes, completely irrational anger.

A demon was always a reflection of sorts of its summoner. And that summoner—a black witch if Sasha's sense of smell was as accurate as usual—was playing with us.

Flynn and Jackson deployed the net. Dark-blue tendrils of power snapped out, wrapping around the demon's hind legs.

The creature opened its many-toothed maw in a mockery of a smile, reached down a three-clawed hand, ripped away a section of the netting, and ate it.

"Lay fire!" Calhoun barked.

The team splintered, tossing a series of pre-made spells in a rapid sequence around the demon. Calhoun deployed his slingshot, hitting the creature dead center between the eyes with three spelled stones in rapid succession.

Fire, edged by sorcerer magic, exploded all around the demon. It reeled back, staggered by Calhoun's headshots.

Then whatever spell coated its scaled hide, whatever allowed it to appear while the sun still hung high in the sky, absorbed the fire. Consumed it. It struck forward with both arms, bellowing its displeasure at whatever pain we'd caused. Its shriek boiled through my mind, frying my brain.

Flynn and Jackson stumbled under the onslaught. The demon knocked them down the rest of the way, sending them flying past me.

I kept running, ducking behind and around Calhoun as he crouched to shoot another series of spells, landing another round of bull's-eyes. Sherwood was tight on my heels.

The demon reared back.

Sasha Piper darted forward and across, scoring its exposed belly with claws and fangs.

Sherwood made a break for the stairs.

I leaped onto the lip of the roof, then onto the top of the exterior stairwell, bringing my blades forward as I took the final leap onto the demon's back.

Its hide was slick with magic. My blades didn't find purchase. I scrambled for footing, wedging my feet against the sharp spurs of its external spine. Then I started to climb toward its head.

It twisted and reared, trying to knock me off. But Flynn and Jackson had rejoined Calhoun and Sasha, and Sherwood was firing from the shelter of the stairwell. The demon was fighting on two fronts.

I reached its head, anchoring my stance as best I could. Then I skewered the demon with both blades, straight into the spot where its brain should have been if the placement of its eyes was any indication.

The creature stilled.

A shudder ran through it.

Then it reached up, grabbed me, and threw me across the roof.

I REGAINED CONSCIOUSNESS WITH CALHOUN, FLYNN, and Jackson huddled around me. I blinked, mentally checking that all my limbs were still attached and in working condition. They hurt, but they moved when commanded. My blades were still in my hands, still tied to my magic, as they would be until I chose to release them.

We were covered in a dome of magic. A shield.

A last resort that most certainly wouldn't hold against the demon for long.

"Sasha?" I asked.

Calhoun's expression tightened, but he kept his gaze on the demon. "X5 pulled you to safe ground, then covered you until we regrouped."

In other words, she hadn't survived protecting me.

I pressed my aching head back against the concrete, fighting a wave of grief that was all my own. X5—Sasha Piper—had spoken of having a family. She'd talked of going hiking in the mountains near her childhood home, of chocolate-and-bacon-flavored ice cream. She had smuggled a green sundress and a mango into the compound two weeks previously, having found both in a local market on our last mission.

She'd brought them for me.

Not only wasn't I allowed out of the compound, I certainly wasn't allowed to wander even when we were working. I wasn't allowed to wear dresses or eat food not supplied by the Collective. Sasha and I had eaten the forbidden fruit in the communal bathroom off the cafeteria, juice running down our fingers while we stifled our laughter. I hadn't even chanced trying on the dress, instead stuffing it under my mattress still in its tight roll.

That night, I'd fallen asleep imagining…imagining the life that dress promised. A life filled with colors and choices. Daily decisions.

Pain surged up in my throat. I choked it back down. Then I pulled myself up into a crouch, casting my gaze around for the demon. "Report," I barked.

"You've been down for about six minutes," Calhoun said, stripping off his gloves. "We're pinned. The demon is badly hurt, but appears to be healing rapidly. We can't cut through the magic coating it with the limited firepower we brought with us. Sherwood made it off the roof, but hunkering down in the stairwell and waiting for us to get him out of the building will be his best bet."

Flynn and Jackson carefully tucked away all their weapons and ammo. Then they also stripped off their gloves.

"We're implementing final protocol," Calhoun said. "The Amplifier Protocol."

I stared at him. Then I glanced down at the bare hands he and the others were holding out to me. I had no idea how Calhoun even knew about the Amplifier Protocol, let alone why he would offer it as a solution.

"Like hell you are," I snarled.

"Amp5…" he started, angry. But then he softened his tone. "Socks. You aren't getting off this roof any other way."

I looked at each of them in turn, incredulous. "So you'd sacrifice yourselves?"

Flynn shrugged his shoulders. "Maybe it won't kill us."

I snapped my teeth shut on an angry retort, on the suggestion that they were anywhere near powerful enough to survive.

I wasn't thinking about the demon, though.

They would have to survive me. Survive what I could do to them.

The Amplifier Protocol was untested. Entirely theoretical. And for good reason. Even if it didn't kill those whose power I was drawing from, no one had any idea what kind of long-term effects it might have. Our trainers weren't certain that even I could survive the massive gathering and casting of magic from multiple sources at once.

"Next suggestion," I said coolly. "The Amplifier Protocol isn't an option."

"It's the only option." Calhoun scrubbed a hand over his face, readying some sort of argument.

I thrust my blades forward in response, sending a pulse of my power through the weapons and slicing through the ward shielding us.

The demon was waiting for me on the other side.

Feeling the shield magic collapsing around me, and blinded by my own rage, I attacked. Whirling, striking. Driving the already wounded demon backward, then to the side. The others joined me, casting the final rounds of their magical arsenal, then making a break for the stairwell door. I had cleared the way to that exit with fierce, efficient brutality.

It helped that I'd already badly wounded the demon. But it wasn't enough.

The demon knocked me down. I rolled under its follow-up strike, seeing Flynn and Jackson make it to the top of the stairs. Flynn was carrying someone. I hoped it wasn't Calhoun.

Claws scored my side. It was just a glancing blow, but agony raked through my torso and I fell to my knees. I rolled forward, between the demon's legs. It lifted a hind foot to crush me.

Magic exploded around its head, from the direction of the exit.

Calhoun.

I looked up. Blood obscured my vision. Evidently I'd hit my head at some point, possibly when the demon had thrown me off its back and knocked me out. I'd reopened the wound, and it was bleeding badly.

The demon swiveled toward Calhoun.

I made it to my feet, stupidly scrambling forward. Stupidly forgetting my training, forgetting everything but the feel of Mark's hands on my skin, drawing pleasure from me…

I shoved Calhoun down into the stairwell, taking the blow intended for him across my back. Screaming, I rolled with the attack, trying to follow Mark through the exit. But the demon stomped down on my legs, breaking both in a fiery agony of pain and pinning me in place.

Then it loomed over me. Leering. Slathering.

It chuckled.

The sound reduced my brain to mush.

The creature flicked its twelve-inch clawed fingers tauntingly in my face, calling my attention back to it. Then it raked those three claws across my stomach.

Again and again.

It punctured my armor.

Over and over.

I screamed. Again and again.

The demon was playing with me.

But there wasn't anything more I could do, trapped and broken beneath it.

I was truly alone. Possibly for the first time in my life.

The pain faded. I didn't wish it back.

Instead, I thought about the comforting feeling of falling asleep every night with Tel5 in my head, even though thick concrete walls and layers of magic separated us. I thought about laughing with Cla5 over some silly joke in a battered children's book. I thought about Nul5 ... the warmth of his hands, feeding his magic with my own need for ... a release—

The demon hooked its claws under my chin. It was crouched over me as if anticipating how it was going to finish me. Then it would eat me, like it had eaten the magical net. It liked to eat magic. And I was exceedingly magical.

But I was too powerful to be eaten. Filled with my blood, my magic, a demon of this magnitude might break free from its summoner.

And if that happened, many, many innocent people would die.

I gurgled up blood, trying to speak. "Come closer, pretty boy."

It leaned in, intent on biting my head off, perhaps.

I stabbed upward with my blades with the last of my strength, the last of my magic. As I skewered the demon's upper palate, its acidic blood spurted all over me. It shrieked, rearing away.

Magic welled up, writhing around the demon. Blood magic, either triggered by the creature's mortal wound or by the summoner if she was in the vicinity, not wanting to lose her pet.

A black sinkhole appeared under the demon, as if the roof had just opened up to the depths of hell. The creature shrieked, reaching its three-clawed fingers for me, trying to pull me with it.

Then it was gone.

Calhoun and the others were shouting, snapping med-spelled wrappings over me. Most likely trying to hold my guts in place.

I didn't look.

I released my blade, lifted my hand, and allowed myself to touch Mark's neck as he leaned over me. Allowing myself the skin-to-skin contact. Just one more time. "I didn't thank you for last night."

He met my gaze, seething in fury. "I think you just did."

I laughed, choking on blood.

Everything went black.

TWO

I WASN'T ON THE ROOF ANYMORE. THE AIR WAS ARTI-
ficially cool. The room around me felt large but empty,
smelling of disinfectant…

I was in a medical facility of some sort. If I'd
been transported all the way to the compound, I'd
definitely lost a chunk of time somewhere along the
way.

I couldn't move. Couldn't open my eyes.

But the pain was gone.

Magic whispered across my mind. A gentle
questing touch. Tel5. She was trying to show me
something telepathically, helping me hear what she
was overhearing.

"She needs to be put down."

A woman. I didn't recognize her voice. And I
wasn't certain who 'she' referred to.

"On what basis, Silver?" The male voice sounded
oddly amplified and muffled at the same time. It was

coming over a speaker. *"Successfully completing her mission? Rescuing me?"*

"I've been telling you, all of you, for years that the empathy is a problem. An unfortunate oversight when we bred her."

"I forbid any unsanctioned action against any of the Five. And especially against Amp5."

Silver laughed coldly. *"And why is that, Azar? Beguiled by those pretty green eyes? Remember we gave those to her."*

"Don't be petty, Silver."

"The Collective will see the incident differently. Amp5 had every opportunity to implement the Amplifier Protocol. That's the action she's been trained to take."

"This wasn't a test. This was an extraction. A successful extraction. The Five functioned exactly as they've been trained to do, including forcing the summoner to withdraw or lose the demon."

Silver snorted, tapping her nails on a hard surface. A table? A desk?

"The shifters shouldn't have gained such easy access to me," Azar said. His tone grew suddenly hard edged. *"And shifters rarely work with witches."*

"Your point?"

"The commanding officer's report indicated that the summoner was a black witch."

"And this is relevant to the issue with Amp5 how?"

"Not in any way, Silver."

"I'm taking the matter to the Collective, Azar. One rotten apple ruins the bunch."

He laughed harshly. "Certainly you aren't suggesting that we wipe out the entire generation?"

"I'm suggesting we have a conversation. We review the situation. And yes, then we reboot."

"Convene the Collective, then. A discussion will be had."

"I'll send out notice today."

"And, Silver? I will also be tabling a resolution suggesting that your tenure as overseer should be shortened, effective immediately. After all, the Five were compromised on your watch…" A soft shifting of sound emanated from the speaker. Azar was flipping through papers on his end of the conversation. "…including Amp5 being attacked by a member of her own team—"

"Simply another example of—"

"Your incompetence."

"You dare, sorcerer?"

The unfinished conversation faded from my mind, as did the comforting feeling of Tel5's presence.

But I knew she was alive. And that she was nearby, if she could pick up and share an overheard conversation between the sorcerer Azar and the current overseer of the Collective, Silver Pine. I hadn't recognized the overseer's voice because I'd never been in the same room as her. But I knew who she was.

I was back in the compound, then. Immobilized somehow, but … aware. For the moment, at least.

One rotten apple ruins the bunch…

I OPENED MY EYES, SLOWLY COMING TO THE REALIZ-ation that I was staring at a white ceiling. I blinked. Steel-caged, flat-mounted light fixtures came into focus. Six of them, evenly spaced. I blinked again. Three sprinklers. An air vent was situated in the upper corner to my right—the most likely place for a hidden camera.

Agony seared across my stomach and lower rib cage.

I gasped.

The skin of my jaw and neck stretched with my involuntary movement. A prickling flush of pain flooded through my head. White dots swam across my eyes.

I inhaled, carefully expanding only my upper ribs. Then I sank into the pain, forcing my body to acknowledge it ... then to disregard it.

The pain, the injuries were insignificant.

Because I was alive.

I would heal.

The agony settled into a dull ache deep within the flesh of my belly that I was certain would flare with the tiniest of movements.

So I didn't move. I closed my eyes, concentrating on breathing shallowly and steadily. Then I opened my mind, feeling for Tel5.

Someone else was in the room with me.

It wasn't one of the Five.

I opened my eyes. Then, as carefully as possible, I turned my head. The skin of my neck and chest—obviously still healing from the demon's acidic blood—protested. I paused, once again willing myself to sink into the pain, claiming it. The searing agony along my jawline dulled.

The bed I was lying in had aluminum rails. Multiple IV poles stood next to me, all of them holding bags filled with different fluids, including blood. I flicked my gaze down my arm without moving my head. I had multiple IV lines attached to my inner elbow, and a monitor on my finger.

I couldn't feel my arm, though its skin bore no sign of damage. I couldn't squeeze my hand to make a fist.

A woman was seated in a chair in the corner, reading a paperback with a sculpted, half-naked male on the cover. Her wavy light-brown hair fell over her brown eyes. She was slim but soft, indicating she wasn't skilled in physical combat. In her midthirties, wearing medium-blue scrubs. A healer, by the tenor of her magic.

The fact that she was monitoring me so closely that she needed to be in the room either meant the Collective expected me to die ... or they expected me to be a problem.

Which meant she was more than a caregiver. More than a healer. Though of course, any healer involved with the Collective was already something more. Someone always willing to go beyond the restrictions enforced by the regulatory bodies of Adept society.

The healer flipped a page in her book, reaching up to toy with her necklace. The silver chain was threaded through a series of carved metal amulets.

Protection spells. Though I couldn't distinguish their specific markings from across the room.

I laughed inwardly. She could shield herself against magical assault easily enough. And maybe even against a telepath or a clairvoyant, if she was highly skilled. But she couldn't ward herself against me, not skin to skin. And her magic worked the same as mine, requiring contact.

She should have heard me gasp. My heart rate would have spiked with the onslaught of pain when I awoke. The monitor was angled toward her.

She should have been on her feet, checking on me, sending in a report that I'd woken.

I closed my eyes, knowing that sleep—true sleep, not simply being knocked out for the pain—was what I needed to heal swiftly. If the healer knew I was awake, she'd increase the sedatives.

I was certain of that. Because the demon on the rooftop in LA had been some sort of test, and it wasn't clear whether I'd passed or failed.

With my future in the balance, with the overseer calling for the Collective to make a ruling, keeping me sedated while I was healing was the logical thing to do.

Eventually, though, my magic would adjust to whatever was in the IV, even if it was a cocktail mixed just for me, for my metabolism. And I didn't doubt that it was exactly that.

The Collective had made certain of my ability to gain an immunity to almost anything magical before I'd even reached maturity. Many Adepts—too many—had died under my unwilling touch before I'd learned how to take what the Collective demanded without killing. I could absorb magic, stripping it so quickly that I caused my victims' hearts to stop, or their brains to simply cease functioning from the trauma.

Still, dying by my hands had to have been more humane than whatever the Collective did to the so-called vessels after I was done harvesting their power. But my empathy—the first power I'd stolen from the first person I'd ever murdered, just by being born—curtailed my ability to be a mass murderer on demand.

I didn't enjoy draining Adepts to the point of killing them. Not even the euphoria of using my inherent magic could fully dampen my empathically triggered conscience.

But rationally?

Rationally, I would always do whatever it took to reach an objective.

So, yes, my healer guard could wear all the protective magic she wanted. But no amulet would protect her from her own ignorance or negligence.

I KEPT MY BREATHING EVEN—AND THEREFORE MY heart rate in check—until I heard the door slide shut behind the healer. She was wearing purple scrubs today. Magic flared around the edges of the door, confirming that I was being sealed into the med bay. Assuming that I was actually being treated at the compound in the first place.

I'd been tracking the healer's movements as regularly as possible between doses of whatever she was using to keep me unconscious. She used a syringe and the IV fluid drip, laying hands on me only in quick, nimble touches as the drug pulled me under. She would check on the progression of my healing, then switch out the bandages if their magic was spent, absorbed by me.

She took three short breaks, each one just after she dosed me, leaving the room for approximately twenty minutes. I'd counted three times to confirm. A male healer took over after twelve hours. Always the same two, rotating shifts.

Without a doubt, the two of them were specialized in the more malignant aspects of healing magic. Just in case I became a problem.

I folded the IV line between two of my fingers the moment the door slid shut, stopping the slow drip. I was becoming less and less affected by the drug, but it wasn't going to be easy to hide my immunity for much longer. Then the healers would either change up the cocktail or transfer me to my room.

My well-secured, impossible-to-break-out-of room.

Once I was there, they had me.

I had no idea if I needed to be concerned. Not yet. I had no concrete understanding of the passage of time. And I hadn't felt the brush of Tel5's thoughts since she'd relayed the conversation between the overseer and Azar.

That was unusual.

Anything unusual when dealing with the Collective was something to monitor, to assess. But I couldn't do that effectively while drugged and confined to a bed.

I sat up carefully so I didn't get tangled in the IV lines. Ignoring the agony screeching through my stomach and lower ribs, I reached over and turned off each of the monitors. I wasn't certain what they tracked, but at least one of them was attached to me and might have thus been alarmed. I removed the IV lines one at a time, gently. Tugging a section of rune-marked adhesive strip from my collarbone, I placed it across my inner elbow, over the needle marks, staunching the pinpoints of blood welling there.

Removing the catheter was an experience I would never need to have again.

Shifting my legs off the edge of the bed proved difficult. And when my hair brushed against my temples, I nearly panicked. For the briefest of moments, I thought I was being attacked. I'd never had hair long enough to fall anywhere near my eyes.

Intense healing might have accelerated hair growth. But even with that factored in, I'd obviously been down for at least a couple of weeks. That was unprecedented. Especially with the power, the magic, that the Collective usually threw at any obstacle.

So was I that badly hurt?

Or had I been deliberately sidelined?

I made it to my feet, feeling the cold of the white-tiled floor. I was naked except for the wide bandage covering my stomach from the lower ribs down to my pelvic bone.

The room sloped almost imperceptibly from all its corners toward a central drain—for hosing down blood and other secretions.

Using one of the IV poles for support, I slowly made it to the second door. The bathroom.

I flicked on the light. I knew that trying to disguise my movements was pointless. Security would eventually pick me up on the cameras, if they hadn't already. But since I was already secured, magically sealed into a room with no weapons of any kind, the protocol would have been to leave me to my own devices unless I tried to harm myself or others.

The woman who looked back at me from the mirror was a stranger. For me, that instinctual reaction wasn't unusual, but it lasted a lot longer than it usually did.

I turned on the tap and ran the cold water. After palming a few sips into my parched mouth, I paused, breathing through waves of pain and disorientation. Too much of the sedative was still in my system for me to move anywhere quickly. But it wasn't enough to dampen the fiery agony that had settled into my stomach.

I'd easily lost five kilos of hard-earned muscle. My already pale skin was a shade much closer to death. My darkly hollowed emerald-green eyes appeared overly large for my face. I looked fevered, though I was starting to shiver.

But whatever damage I'd sustained to my face and neck from the demon's acidic blood had healed completely.

My stomach started cramping in response to the rapid water consumption, so I stopped drinking even though I was still thirsty. Then I turned, angling my head and twisting my shoulders so I could catch sight in the mirror of the four blood tattoos situated at the center of my upper back. One on each of my first four thoracic vertebrae.

The tattoos glowed softly despite the harsh glare of the bathroom lights. One for each of the other four.

Designations: Nul5, Tel5, Cla5, and Tek5. Nicknamed by Cla5 before we'd all reached our third birthdays, from a series of children's books—Fish, Bee, Knox, and Zans. I was Fox in Socks, shortened to Socks.

Nul5's blood—Fish's blood—was magically bound to my T1 vertebra so that he could access it by touch if necessary, even if I was wearing armor.

My blood, my magic, had been bound to the other four in that exact same spot, and for the same reason.

I hadn't been able to access and amplify Fish's nullifying power before we'd all been tattooed. That was the nature and purpose of his magic—to nullify any and all energy he came in contact with, including my amplification. But after he'd been linked to me through the blood tattoos, he was able to generate massive mobile shields that nullified any magical or energy-based effect thrown his way. The Collective had been thrilled at that development of our abilities.

Bee was tied to my T2 vertebra, giving the telepath unhindered access to my mind. I couldn't block Tel5 from my thoughts even if I wanted to.
"
Knox's clairvoyance was bound to my T3. Cla5 and I were most often paired together in situations that called for strategic manipulation. Clandestine missions with the clairvoyant situated offsite, whispering directions through his glimpses of my future in my ear.

Zans's blood and power were tied to my T4 vertebra, but it was most often Tek5 who drew from my amplification abilities, rather than me drawing from her telekinesis.

Relief flooded through me at the sight of the glow that edged each tattoo. I hadn't known, hadn't realized how concerned I was for the others. Without Bee's near-constant presence in the back of my mind, I'd thought that the telepath might be dead. But I was fairly certain that the tattoos would have faded if one of us ever died, because our power, our magic, our essence would vanish with us.

So whatever was dampening our connection was magical. And therefore deliberate. An intentional separation.

That didn't necessarily indicate that the Collective had ruled against me, though. For all I knew, the other four might have been just as badly hurt as I was. The conversation that Bee had relayed between the overseer, Silver Pine, and the sorcerer we'd rescued, Kader Azar, might simply have been a random, unintentional connection. The telepath could have been in a med bay right next to mine and as heavily sedated as I was, but without my eventual immunity to such things.

My legs started shaking. I sat on the toilet, catching my breath. Then I willed myself to pass some urine so I could check it for blood. Urinating stung, but the water in the bowl remained practically clear.

So I was well hydrated.

Still perched on the toilet, I ran my fingers over the rune-covered bandages mummifying me from just below my breasts to an inch from my pubic bone, finding their edges. The magic peeled away with a warm prickle, exposing three large puffy red slashes across my body from my lower left rib to my upper right hip. The wounds had been stitched together.

Stitched. With thick black thread.

Stitches.

I'd never needed anything so mundane to aid in my healing.

The demon had eaten magic. Literally. So perhaps its claws functioned similarly?

I remembered it tearing into me, over and over until it had finally punctured armor that had been created to impede any spell, blade, or bullet. So had it destroyed or consumed my magic as well?

I was going to scar. Rather dramatically. The idea was disconcerting on a completely irrational, emotional level.

My soul was already in tatters.

Why shouldn't my body reflect it?

But I was alive.

For now.

I rewrapped the bandages, though the adhesive didn't stick as well the second time. The magic threaded through the wrappings eased some of the burning sensation that had flared when I uncovered the claw wounds.

I ran my shaking fingers through my hair. It was silky, soft. A deep-red color that looked fake.

But it was me. Mine.

The Collective would make me shave my head before my next mission. An order would be issued, handed down, before I was released back to my room. One of the healers would do it while I sat quietly, obediently.

And in response to that thought, an idea that wouldn't be quashed, wouldn't be brushed away, bloomed in the back of my mind.

What gave the Collective the right?

Other than breeding, housing, training, and feeding me?

I laughed, a quiet sound. But it stirred up enough residual pain from my wounds to take my breath away.

I was theirs. That was what gave them the right. The Collective owned me, body and soul. And if they decided that I was expendable, as the overheard conversation between the overseer and the sorcerer Azar suggested? Well… that idea was preposterous, actually. I was a valued asset, as were the others. I would heal, and the Collective would… recondition me if they deemed any action necessary. And then we'd be as we always were.

Highly skilled, highly trained servants of destruction.

I ran my hand through my hair again, playing with it. It was silly to attach such importance to a few inches of hair. Completely illogical.

But again, I couldn't shake the unsettled feeling. The instinctual need to… what? Fight back? Demand that I not be shorn? Withhold my services?

I still had too many drugs in my system. They were affecting my judgement, muddying my rational, logical assessment of the situation.

The door swooshing open in the main room announced the return of the healer.

I used the edge of the sink to get to my feet, holding myself aloft and steadily meeting her dark-eyed gaze as she stepped into the doorway. Naked and half-dead or not, I'd be on my feet to meet her.

I was someone to be feared. It was best she knew that.

It was harder to try to kill someone who terrified you. In theory.

Dark-blond streaks that looked artificial were threaded through her light-brown hair. She stood five inches shorter than my five-foot-ten.

"You've been playing possum," she said. Her tone was neutral, lightly accented American. "And you thought I didn't know."

"I have no need of the sedatives," I said. "They impede my healing."

A flash of anger marred her pleasant features. Then she smoothed the emotion away. "The level of pain you must be experiencing impedes your healing."

I softened my tone, offering her a touch of a smile. "You've done admirably."

She looked pleased for a moment. Then she narrowed her eyes.

"No more sedatives," I said, not bothering with playing nice. I didn't have the energy or the temperament to pull it off.

"Vitamins—"

"Orally will be fine. There's no need for the IV ... or the catheter." I stepped forward, crowding her until she shifted back. "Take it up the line." Propping myself up in the doorframe, I scanned the room, making eye contact with the nearest air vent and hoping that one of my team members was on duty. However many of them were left. "No more sedatives. This is a formal request. Take it all the way up the line."

"I heard you the first time," the healer said from behind me.

Ignoring her, I slowly made my way back to the bed. Then I ruined all my posturing by collapsing, slamming my chin with the full force of my weight on the side railing, and falling onto the tiled floor.

The healer stepped closer, peering down smugly. "If your goal was to reopen the wounds, you've achieved it."

I didn't manage a comeback. Possibly because it felt as though I might have broken my jaw. But I tried to hold off the blackness edging my vision until she touched me. I didn't need words to wipe the superior look off her face.

Unfortunately, the blackness won.

THE NEXT TIME I WOKE, I WAS STRAPPED TO THE BED, though there was no IV stuck in my arm. So I'd conquered one hurdle only to find myself hampered by another. Bothersome. But not unexpected.

Since there was no point in pretending to be asleep anymore, I scanned the room. A slight, dark-skinned male was tapping on a tablet in the corner chair. The second healer. His ears were pierced, four amulets in each, laced with protection spells.

"Water, please."

He started, then immediately rose to cross over to me, picking up and offering me a white plastic cup with a straw.

I made a show of awkwardly getting the straw in my mouth. Then I sipped the ice water, blinking as if not completely clearheaded.

Which I wasn't.

His light-brown-eyed gaze snagged on my mouth, watching me with more than the detached reserve of a caregiver.

Though that could have meant anything, really. It was my magic that was beguiling, not me.

I didn't like playing at being helpless. But I also didn't like being strapped to the bed. It was difficult to act intimidating while tied up.

I rested my head back on the pillow, blinking at him sleepily. "Thank you."

He nodded, setting down the water and angling his shoulders to check the monitors, all of which were back on.

I twisted my wrists in the restraints, checking my own strength. I was weak. As expected.

"Oh," I said softly. "Did I fall?"

"Ah…" He cleared his throat. "Yes." He wore short-sleeved, dark-blue scrubs, no gloves. He held the bulk of his power in the palms of his hands, which made sense for a healer.

The bare skin was a risky choice around me. Though not so much while I was restrained.

I allowed my eyes to flutter closed, then open again. "I don't recognize you," I murmured.

He leaned over me, a curl of a smile at the edges of his lips. "I'm new. The name is Brad."

"And my team, Brad?" I let my voice catch, as if overwhelmed. "Have they ... did they?"

"I know that you're the only one in the hospital wing. So if anyone else was brought in with you, they're not here now."

"Oh ... thank you for telling me."

"How's the pain?"

Horrendous. "Manageable."

"Can you stomach some food?"

Food sounded like a terrible idea. "Um, something ... light. Toast?"

"Buttered?"

"Yes, please. But just lightly, and completely melted."

He chuckled as if I was adorable, crossing to the intercom by the door. "Of course."

He turned his back to me, placing an order for lightly buttered toast, a banana, and apple juice.

I quickly glanced around the room, confirming that there was nothing nearby that could be used to cut through my bonds. There wasn't even a set of drawers at hand in which something useful might have been stored. The only weapons I'd have access to in the med bay would have to be repurposed. The IV stand, if I could snap it in half. The metal legs of the chair, if I could remove them.

If ... if ... if I wasn't strapped to the bed. If I wasn't so weak.

If I even needed to escape.

But the overheard conversation between the overseer and the sorcerer Azar still haunted my thoughts. I knew that it might have just been some dream, some hallucination pulled forth out of my ingrained fear of never being good enough. The newly unpleasant notion that I was expendable. But even if so, the absence of the others bothered me. If Bee was okay, then why wasn't she in my head?

Something was definitely going on.

Even if I could get out of the room, though, and even if I managed to make it out of the hospital wing, there was no escaping the compound. I wouldn't make it up or down a single level, not if the Collective didn't want me going anywhere.

The healer stepped to the side of the bed. "Everything okay? You look … tense."

"Just worried about the others."

He nodded, leaning over the side rail. "May I take your pulse?"

He was asking permission to touch me—while I was awake and aware.

That didn't make any sense.

"Yes."

The healer brushed his fingers against my bare wrist. I forced my arm to remain limp, keeping my magic tightly in check. I watched him for any twitch, any sign that he was about to try to murder me.

He smiled, glancing at the watch on his opposite wrist. "You were right about the sedation," he said conversationally. "You're healing much better now."

He pressed something into the palm of my hand. A flat disc of metal, approximately an inch and a half in diameter.

I curled my fingers around the disc, feeling the magic contained within it tickle my palm. I made no other reaction.

"Good," he said, dropping my wrist. "Solid. Steady." He reached for the water, offering it to me again.

I sipped it without pretense. I didn't need to figure him out or try to play him. He'd already been recruited by one of the Five, likely Bee or Knox. Both were far better with people than I was.

"We'll get you something to eat," he said. "And then I suggest you nap. Yes?"

I nodded, understanding that the suggested nap was likely to trigger the magic in the disc I held. I took another sip of water and tried to be patient.

BEFORE I COULD FIGURE OUT WHAT THE PURPOSE OF the disc was, Brad fed me. Annoyingly. He would have been under orders to not let me out of the restraints, and with the cameras on us, hand feeding me was his only choice.

So I ate, hoping the water or the food weren't laced with sedatives.

They weren't.

Then Brad settled into the far corner of the room with his tablet, and I willed myself to sleep.

THREE

"IT TOOK YOU LONG ENOUGH," BEE SAID PEEVISHLY. "I had to make Brad think I'd blown him three times. There was actual touching involved the last time. Ugh."

I opened my eyes, finding myself surrounded by white walls. My feet felt the sensation of a polished concrete floor. A drain was barely hidden underneath the neatly made single bed. Light-gray wool blanket, white sheets.

A twin to my room in the compound.

I was wearing a gray tank top and matching sweatpants. Both were slightly too large, though not enough that they would impede my movements.

If I could move.

Which, it appeared, I couldn't.

"Socks?" Bee asked in my mind. *"Can you hear me?"*

A colorful rug appeared under my feet, with matching throw pillows suddenly scattered across the bed. A black-and-white photograph of a sunflower appeared on the wall. Only the single bee captured within the image was allowed any color, its black contrasting with vibrant yellow as the insect collected pollen from the flower.

I was standing in Tel5's room. Well, Bee's room as it appeared in the telepath's mind.

"Ah, there you are."

Bee appeared, cross-legged at the center of the bed. Her yellow-blond hair was long, tucked behind her ears, brushing her shoulders. She was wearing a tunic over leggings in dark shades of green. Her light-brown eyes and naturally tanned skin were authentic, but the rest was a projection of herself. Apparently, Bee wanted long hair today, and clothing that came in colors, and a vibrant rug in the middle of her room.

The photograph on the wall might have been my own manifestation. A way for my mind to comprehend visiting a telepath in a construct of her own mind, her magic.

A tingling in my arms told me that I'd be able to move them now. I raised them before me, stretching and flexing my fingers, though the action didn't come particularly easily.

Bee frowned. "You were hurt. Badly. They actually brought in outside healers. They've kept you under so deeply that I haven't been able to establish contact firmly enough to bring you here."

"I took care of the sedation, so the med bay might be shielded against you." I rolled my neck, then my shoulders. Gently, carefully, I lifted one leg, then the other. The polished concrete in my mind firmed under my feet, anchoring me further into Bee's mentally constructed space.

"Well…" Bee sneered. "That can be turned against them, can't it?"

It was a rhetorical question. All magic could be turned against its user, whether offensive or defensive power. All of the Five were particularly capable of subverting magic. Doing so was a fundamental function of the abilities that made me more than simply a powerful amplifier. "They brought unvetted healers to the compound? Brad said he was new."

"Not that new." Bee waved her hand. "Before that. Before they brought you back. Although…" She tilted her head questioningly. "There was a moment, when Knox and I found you on the roof, when Calhoun was threatening…"

She didn't finish the thought. Instead, her gaze went remote. "Ah…"

Tek5 appeared at the foot of the bed. The telekinetic's fists were clenched, anger etched across her face. Zans was dressed similarly to me. The light-gray sweats were a deep contrast to her dark-brown skin. Her hair was clipped short, as usual.

"Stop that," Bee said mildly.

Zans shot the telepath a look.

"You know I can't hold you here if you fight me."

"I'm not fighting," Zans spat. She turned her ire on me. "I thought you were dead!"

The photograph of the sunflower and the bee above and behind Tel5 started to vibrate, then shake.

Zans disappeared.

Bee sighed. "Maybe we'll let her cool off."

Magic ghosted across my back as Knox stepped into the mental construct. An echo of his hand slid across my back and up my arm, cupping my neck. Taking liberties he'd never dare to in person. I touched few people, and rarely made contact with the clair-voyant. Our magic wasn't compatible at all.

"Fox in Socks," he whispered, curling his fingers under my chin as if he could actually touch me, could actually turn my head toward him.

I obliged him as I never did in person, turning to meet his light-gray eyes. We were almost the same height, him slightly taller than me. His white-blond hair was so short that it was just an absence of color when compared to his golden skin. He was paler than normal, dark circles under his eyes.

I looked at Bee sharply, drawing conclusions based on Cla5's pallor. "You were hurt."

"It was nothing," Knox said, stepping away from me and settling on the bed beside Bee. He was wearing sweats but his feet were bare, as was usual. "Nothing compared to the injuries you sustained."

"We experienced some … interference," Bee said. "Our team was hit hard. Taken out."

"All of them?"

Tension ran through Knox's jaw. He nodded curtly. The clairvoyant had never lost a member of his immediate team. Ever. Not in dozens of missions, and not in any of our no-rules training sessions either.

"Another telepath?"

Knox and Bee glanced at each other, but it was Bee who answered. "We don't know."

That gave me pause. Each of the Five wielded unique abilities. The idea that someone, anyone, could have overcome both Cla5 and Tel5 was ... well, impossible.

That was becoming a running motif. A series of disconnected observations that were adding up to a conclusion I didn't particularly like.

Who knew the Five well enough—both individually, and as a team—that they could have compromised us so thoroughly? Including convincing one of the members of my own team to try to kill me if I appeared to be accomplishing my mission.

"Were you sleeping with X4?" I asked. "Tom Hannigan?"

"No." Knox grinned. "But then, he never asked."

Bee snorted, then she wagged her eyebrows at me. "I wouldn't call it sleeping."

I nodded grimly.

"Why, Socks?" Bee asked. "And why ask in the past tense? Is ... do you think Tom was involved?"

"I know he was."

She clenched her fists. "That's ... that's..."

"Impossible?"

"Nothing is impossible," Knox whispered.

"He's dead, then?" Bee asked bluntly. "You killed him for betraying us?"

Mark Calhoun had been the one to pull the trigger, twice. But I would take any retribution Bee might be inclined to dole out. "Yes."

She nodded, lowering her gaze to her clasped hands.

The mental construct shifted under my feet. I took a deep and steady breath, relishing the fact that my wound didn't scream with pain as I filled my illusory lungs. I probably had Bee to thank for that. Left to my own devices, I would have brought the pain with me, as I had the ill-fitting clothing and the bandages that swathed my lower torso.

Knox moved to settle his arm across Bee's back.

"No!" she snarled. "Hannigan was just a game anyway. He means … meant nothing to me."

Knox dropped his arm, looking to me, looking for me to get us through the moment. As I had always done. As I would always do. That was another one of my roles, though it remained unspoken between the five of us.

"Shall we continue?" I asked, keeping my tone steady and dispassionate. The mystery of Tom Hannigan's betrayal—and of who might be capable of creating an amulet powerful enough to fool Bee's telepathy—wasn't going to be solved standing around in a mental construct. "You've brought me here. You need something from me?"

"Yes," Bee said. Firming her tone, she repeated, "Yes. And we're taking too much time. Even with you anchoring it, the focal spell I had Brad give you isn't going to last more than an hour. And, honestly, I don't think I can stand to spend any more time in his head."

"No more blow jobs?" Knox asked teasingly. "Poor guy."

"Please," Bee spat. "You know the types of healers the Collective employs. I'm surprised they can even stand to be in their own heads."

The room settled as Bee refocused. The edges of the walls sharpened, and the concrete firmed under my feet again.

"You could have just forced him," Knox said gently.

"No." Bee shook her head. "It hasn't come to that yet."

Bee wasn't just a powerful telepath. As with my own magic, as with the rest of the Five, she'd been bred to be Tel5—far more than a mind reader. She could manipulate people, planting thoughts and suggestions. If she needed to, she could get deep enough into someone's head that she could completely wipe everything that made them who they were. Every memory, every thought. She could create living, breathing zombies that did her bidding.

And each time she did, it shredded her soul. Every person she'd murdered under orders while we'd been training, whether their bodies still functioned when she was done or not.

Same as me.

Same as any of us.

And we never talked about it. Not even in this place. Not even in Bee's mind, away from the cameras and the twenty-four-hour surveillance.

Nul5 appeared by the door, eyeing me coolly. The dark-haired nullifier was dressed in standard gray sweats, though his T-shirt stretched tightly enough across his broad shoulders that he really needed a larger size.

"Took you long enough," he snapped at Bee, though his brown-eyed gaze remained on me. He was the only one of the Five with a hint of Asian ancestry in his features, though the physical markers weren't distinct enough to make any actual guesses as to his heritage.

Because our genetic materials had never mattered. Only the combination of power signatures that came with them.

"You know I couldn't pull you in until you fell asleep, Fish," Bee huffed.

It was my turn to frown. That wasn't right. I might have been behind some sort of ward meant to block telepathy, hence my need for the focal amulet. But the Five were tied together through the blood tattoos. Tel5 didn't even need physical contact to talk to more than one of us at a time. She'd successfully contacted me from over forty kilometers away in field tests. The Collective had yet to find a need to push her any farther than that, so we had no idea of her true range.

"They've separated you? Secured your rooms? You're under lockdown?"

"Yeah," Fish spat. "They've separated us. No contact with each other. And our movements are being restricted. Just in case you wondered why you haven't had any visitors."

"I hadn't been."

He snarled. "Of course you haven't. Because you expect nothing of us. Because none of us measures up to you, oh empath."

"Actually, I haven't been conscious long enough to have visitors."

Knox laughed quietly to himself.

"Where's Tek5?" Fish growled, turning away from me resolutely. "Let's get this over with."

"She got too angry," Bee said. "Probably woke herself up."

Fish, aka Nul5, scrubbed his hands over his face and shaved head. "How much does Amp5 know?"

The trio turned to look at me, which wasn't unusual. I was the center pin of the Five. At some point in each of our missions, in each of our training exercises, they all had to defer to me. They just didn't have to enjoy it. Fish was older than me by six months, so my position, which was due to my magical abilities, had bothered him since we'd been children.

We weren't children now, though.

And honestly, in that moment, it grated on me to hear him call me 'Amp5.' I wasn't much a fan of simply being a designation, and I could tolerate the nicknames Knox had given us all when we were only toddlers. But I'd never understood why remaining nameless made me more malleable in my handlers' minds. Was it supposed to be easier to strip people of their magic, to amplify others with that stolen magic, to maim and murder, without a name?

Who had decided that?

"It's too soon," Knox said quietly, his light-gray eyes searching my face. "Socks is still healing."

"Well, there's an easy fix to that, isn't there?" Fish muttered caustically.

This was one of those moments, those moments that I would never really figure out until after it had passed. Until I saw the behavior reflected by those who moved around us, or in a book or a movie we watched or read when we were away from the compound. In the rare instance we were at the edge of the Collective's reach.

I was supposed to offer comfort. I was supposed to soothe Fish. I was supposed to apologize, to make everything better.

But why that task fell to me, I didn't know. In fact, I was fairly certain that it was my empathy that had everyone all riled up. So why they demanded that I use that same capacity to soothe them was a mystery.

Still, time was short. "Did you project the conversation between the overseer and the sorcerer Azar?" I asked Bee.

She nodded. "I didn't know if you picked it up."

"Some, at least. Did the overseer enforce the curfew and lockdown before or after that?"

"After." Fish started pacing. If we hadn't been in Bee's mental space, his magic would have been creeping across the floor, chilling my feet, numbing me.

Faced with that possibility, I came to a sudden realization.

I didn't want to be numbed. Not anymore.

"Has the Collective convened?"

"We don't know," Bee said.

"We don't care," Knox added.

I eyed each of them in turn, already knowing what they wanted from me. And I'd been wrong. It wasn't to be soothed.

I glanced down at my hands, at my bare arms, pressing my palms lightly against my stomach. "How hurt was I? How long have I been bedridden?"

"Hurt enough that you have to ask," Fish said angrily.

But he wasn't angry at me. It had taken me some time to work that out. They were all angry, but not at me.

"Sixty-seven days," Bee said.

I closed my eyes. Sixty-seven days. With all the magic at the Collective's disposal? With all the stolen magic in my veins, embedded in my tissue, skewered through my heart and soul? No wonder they were concerned for me. And for their own lives. "That was one hell of a demon," I whispered.

I'd been completely unprepared to face such an opponent. And judging by the way I'd been cut off from the others, that had been the entire point.

I was supposed to have died in LA. The mission was meant to have failed. But whether that was because of me specifically or if the Five had gotten caught up in some plot against the sorcerer Azar, I had no idea and no way of figuring out.

Except now we were experiencing ongoing repercussions. Separating us even more than we were usually kept apart. Drugging me, bringing in healers I didn't recognize. Hindering any chance that I'd develop any sort of personal connection with my caregivers.

All of that felt a lot like a target on my forehead.

But why wait? Why bring me back to the compound at all? Factions within factions? Was there a schism happening among the Collective? And if so, who was on which side? The overseer pitted against the sorcerer Azar? Was the kidnapping tied to the demon on the roof, or had the demon simply been an extra test for me?

There was no way to know, no way to collect enough information. And knowing anything for certain wouldn't actually change the situation anyway. It wouldn't change my reaction, or the results of any action I might need to take.

I opened my eyes. "Get Zans."

Bee nodded, closing her own eyes even though she was just a projection of her physical self.

"We have time," Knox said.

"Time enough that you haven't seen what happens?" I asked. "No hints? No glimmers?"

He shook his head.

Typically, Knox's clairvoyance gave him glimpses into the immediate future, but occasionally he saw more. Forty-six hours was the longest we'd tracked. Dampening his magic was obviously possible. But he would feel and recognize the effects, even those of a subtle spell. Because his magic always simmered, constantly tapping into future echoes that he'd learned to ignore. And we had all felt the psychic assault on the rooftop.

Zans appeared on the rug in front of me. She was cross-legged, attempting to meditate. She opened her eyes, glancing around, then nodding. "Where are we at?"

"We were just explaining to Amp5 that she needs to get out of that damn bed and break us out," Fish said.

His request settled across my shoulders like a weighted blanket. I brushed off the sensation as a side effect of being in Bee's mind construct. Words, requests, didn't carry weight.

Zans rolled to her feet, pacing around me. Assessing me. "She's still healing."

"And we have things to plan." Bee unfolded her legs, stepping forward so that she stood in the center, ringed by all of us. "Things that need to be put in place."

"Plan?" Fish echoed. "While locked in our rooms?"

"Try to not be a continual idiot, Nul5," Zans snapped. "We get plenty of time out, just not at the same time. As far as Bee has picked up, the Collective hasn't even convened."

"You ... you really think they're done with us?" I whispered. A dread that I wanted to deny but couldn't shake seeped into my chest. "Done with the entire fifth generation?"

"You showed your true colors in LA, Amp5." Fish crossed his arms.

"I've done the same many, many times. Getting my team off the roof was a rational decision."

"If you'd been backed by one or more of us, then yes," Knox said quietly. "But with only your immediate team, faced with a greater demon, you should have ... sacrificed them. Harvested their magic and dealt with the demon yourself."

"Murdered them," I said. "Let's be clear. You wanted me to murder people who have fought at our sides, protected us with their lives, for years, just to pass some sort of test?"

"Yes," Nul5 spat.

Bee raised her hand, silencing Fish. "What do you mean 'a test'?"

"That's what it was, wasn't it? What did the sorcerer say? An unsanctioned test?"

"No. He didn't. He used the word unsanctioned when talking about ... eliminating you."

I frowned.

"It was a test," Tek5 said. Her tone was hollow, as if she was just putting everything together. "One we all failed."

They all turned to me again. Concerned. Confused.

"We wait," I said. "Trying to break out of the compound would be ridiculous. If we're still concerned, we abort the next mission."

"That could be months from now," Fish said.

"We've got time—"

"Socks!" Fish snarled. He attempted to punch a hole in the concrete wall. A wall that didn't actually exist.

"Ow," Bee said, pouting playfully. Though Fish's nullifying magic might have actually hurt her even within her own construct. We Five were tied together that tightly.

"You put us here." Fish stepped up to me, standing too close. "You forced this point. Without including us in your decisions." His lips lined up with my nose.

I didn't step back. I never did. And I wasn't going to start now.

"You will do whatever is necessary to get us out," he snarled.

I angled my head, meeting his eyes. After a moment, he grimaced, looking away from me, then back again.

"I have always done whatever is necessary." I spoke quietly, pointedly. "But I refuse to be hasty. To make decisions based on suppositions."

"You'll know when they come for us," Fish said, matching my cool tone. "They'll wait until we're locked in. And none of us is immune to whatever they'll choose to pump in. Not even me. Not even you." Fish gestured to a vent in the corner of the illusory room. It wasn't just there for air circulation.

We'd been locked in our separate rooms numerous times growing up. Usually when one of us was being punished, or they were making adjustments to our training regimens.

But the last time they'd sedated us with gas had been over six years before. I'd been a couple of weeks shy of fifteen when I'd started menstruating, later than both Bee and Zans. The Collective had been waiting for me to reach maturity in order to harvest my blood. Not that I'd known that at the time.

When I'd woken up back in my bed, the only evidence I had of anything happening at all was the four blood tattoos along my spine. Tattoos we'd all woken up with, inked in each other's blood, anchoring our magic to each other. That was what allowed us to gather in Bee's mind, or for me to reach through and past Fish's ability to nullify magic. That was what directed Knox's visions, firmly focusing them on the Five.

"Socks," Fish snapped. "We can't get out of our rooms on our own. If they gas us, we're done."

"That'll never happen," I said evenly. "We're valuable resources. If they have a problem with me, they'll come for me. And me alone."

"And what?" Zans asked. "Add a new amplifier to the group?"

"Yes. Or other team members. You would adapt, be retrained. Same as what would happen if one of us died on mission."

"Please," she spat. "One of us, maybe. Not you."

"Procedure dictates—"

"Socks! That's never going to happen. If they come for you, they'll come for all of us."

One rotten apple ruins the bunch.

I shook my head, denying the echo of the overseer's words and Zans's assertion at the same time. "The sorcerer Azar said that he'd have me know him. If the demon and compromising the team was a test, he wasn't involved."

Fish laughed nastily. "Just because he wants to fuck you doesn't mean he'll stand against the Collective. Hell, it was probably all bullshit. What are the chances a sorcerer of any power could have been taken by a bunch of rogue shapeshifters?"

"Rogue shifters backed by a black witch of immense power," Knox said mildly. "To have the ability to call a greater demon."

"In the daylight," Bee added.

"Kader Azar." I glanced over at Bee. "That was who was conversing with Silver Pine. Was it a phone call you overheard?"

She nodded.

"I recognized his voice."

"And she named him," Bee said. "How many members of the Collective does that make now? Five? And the names we know? Silver Pine—"

"Not important," Zans interrupted. "We have plans to make." She turned to look at me. "We have to be ready. That means healing, Socks. Quickly."

I nodded, ignoring the chill that ran up my arms over what she was asking me to do. "If it becomes necessary."

A fierce smile spread across Zans's face. "We aren't going quietly," she said. Almost conversationally.

"I doubt that will be an option."

"You know what I mean," she snarled. "I'm taking it all down, Socks. And you four are going to help me do it."

I opened my mouth to answer but Zans disappeared with an audible pop.

Bee sighed heavily. "She keeps waking herself. Having you all in my head is no party. I'm getting a serious migraine."

"We need a plan," I said, feeling the mental construct waver and shift. "We'll need transportation, passports, money. If we get out."

"Just wake the fuck up, Socks," Fish said. "Come for us. We'll sort everything else out."

I opened my mouth to argue. I wasn't going to make a hasty escape. I wasn't going to rush into—

Fish disappeared, then Knox, then Bee.

I opened my eyes. I was back in my hospital bed. Still shackled. Pain seared across my stomach, radiating through my torso, chest, and limbs. And for a moment, it took my breath, my resolve, with it.

I lay there, suffering silently.

Trapped.

My agony was a physical manifestation of what I'd always endured.

Caged.

As I'd always been. Just much, much more obviously now.

FOUR

THEY'RE COMING. SOCKS! WAKE UP! THEY'RE COMING for you.

Adrenaline, triggered by the terror that flooded through Bee's abrupt telepathic wake-up call, washed through my system. I woke, gasping and rearing forward in the bed.

I was still shackled to the railings. The female healer was hovering beside me, a needle in one hand.

She laughed, nervous and trying to hide it. "Bad dream?"

I raised my forearms, testing my strength and the range of the shackles. I had about five inches of play, but I hadn't regained enough strength to wrench open the clasps or tear the straps.

"Everything okay?" the healer asked. Her gaze flicked to my tethered arms in concern.

Everything was fine. She should have limited my range even more.

"What's your name?" I asked. My voice was thick with emotion not wholly my own. Residual from Bee.

"Excuse me?"

"Your name?" I growled, my eyes settling on the needle in her hand. "If you're going to try to kill me, I deserve your name, don't I?"

She laughed again, the sound stuttering out. "You had a bad dream, Amp5. This is simply a broad-spectrum antibiotic. I'm worried about your wound—"

"It's been over two months. If an infection was going to set in, it would have done so."

"Oh, you're a doctor now? I didn't realize that you gained universal knowledge along with the superpowers they gave you."

I pinned her with my gaze. "It's going to be difficult to prick me with that tiny needle when I'm awake."

"Now you're just being silly." She made a show of lifting her hands before her, then turning to place the needle in a rolling metal tray beside the bed. Three more capped syringes were neatly lined in a row on the tray. All of that was new.

Three more syringes. Four in total. They weren't sure how difficult it was going to be to kill me. Good to know.

"Are you operating on directives from the Collective?" I asked, slowly twisting my wrists in the restraints.

"Of course," the healer huffed.

"Verbal orders or sealed paper?"

She snapped her mouth closed, crossing her arms.

I laughed. "A kill order always comes magically sealed, signed by a quorum."

She turned away, glancing up toward the camera behind the vent in the corner. Yeah, it was probably time to implement plan B. Which meant I needed to move.

I gathered my legs underneath me, awkwardly pulling them out from under the tightly tucked covers.

"You're going to reopen your wounds," the healer said peevishly.

"Yes," I said calmly. "Most likely. But don't worry, it'll heal quickly. And this would all go much more smoothly if you told me your name."

"Right. If I tell you my name, then you'll let me take care of you properly?"

I laughed harshly. "No. If you tell me your name, I might feel badly about killing you. I might even remember killing you."

"You're just as bad as the rest of them," she snarled.

The intercom beside the door flashed. She crossed toward it, turning her back to palm the button. "Yes?"

Idiot.

Pulling my knee tightly to my chest and angling my upper body as far away as I could, I slammed my foot into the left-side railing of the bed.

She spun back, eyes wide.

A second kick and a harsh yank freed my left arm.

A voice came over the intercom. "Your presence is required in room C."

The healer dove for the tray beside the bed, going for the needles.

I kicked her in the stomach, tumbling half off the bed as I did so. My right arm was still bound to the other railing.

She doubled over, stumbling into the tray and sending it spiraling across the room. All four syringes scattered across the white tile.

Pain raked through my guts. I hung from the bed, panting.

The healer stumbled away from me, eyeing the nearest syringe but going for the door. She passed her hand over the door lock's palm reader. The lock blinked red.

She tried again. Red.

Again. Red.

I laughed, sliding back up onto the bed so I could reach across and loosen the other restraint. "Now would be a really good time to tell me your name. Whoever you've got in security monitoring us isn't going to let you out. In fact, I'm guessing they're going up the line for the okay to gas us both."

She turned to look at me. Angry, not scared.

I made it to my feet, stumbling. I caught myself on the bed.

"Please," she said with a sneer, skirting the wall toward the nearest syringe. "You're half starved. You've been in that bed for over two months. If you were something to be afraid of, you would have acted by now."

I rested, allowing her the time to get her hands on the syringe. She crouched, picking it up. She stepped toward me.

"You're going to need more than one," I said, nodding toward the next nearest syringe. It had rolled under the chair in the far corner.

More anger flitted across her face, but she stepped back and collected the syringe, then gathered the last two from near the bathroom door. She tucked three needles in her pocket, uncapping the fourth.

"Why the needles?" I asked conversationally, pressing my hand against the slash wounds across my stomach. I hadn't reopened them yet, but they hurt. "I would have thought you were one of those healers who kill with just a touch. Otherwise they wouldn't have put you in here ... with someone like me."

"It's a sedative. I do plan on killing you myself. I was thinking a heart attack or a brain aneurism. But now I think I'll torture you for a bit."

I laughed. "While I'm sedated? That will be terribly ineffective."

She snarled, crossing toward me with purpose.

"You should be wearing more clothing," I said.

Her step hitched. "What?"

"Nothing. I only need an inch or so anyway. So it really doesn't matter."

She raised her hand, needle at the ready.

I waited, slumped on the bed.

She lunged.

I straightened, spun around her outstretched hand, reached up and grabbed a fistful of her hair at the back of her head.

She shrieked indignantly.

I pressed her against me, pinning her arm, then twisting her wrist sharply.

She dropped the needle at her feet.

"Sorry," I whispered. "No time to sedate you."

"Macy," she cried. Her terror zinged through me, picked up by my frequently maligned empathy. "My name ... my name..."

I tore her magic from her fiercely, channeling it into myself.

She sucked in a pained breath, sagging against me.

I took more. I took it all. All of the healing power that resided in every cell of her body, that flowed through her veins. I already had the ability to kill by touch, but I wasn't trying to cast with her magic. I couldn't actually wield stolen power, not without keeping in contact with the vessel.

I dropped Macy at my feet, leaving her gasping, likely dying.

I allowed the stolen magic to slip through me, healing myself as much as I could with her power. I peeled the bandages from my torso, finding raw-looking, light-pink scar tissue where the stitched wounds had been.

Macy was trying to speak, trying to reach for me. Begging, maybe.

I grabbed the sheet, ripping it into strips as I stepped over the healer and crossed to the door. I eyed the intercom and the door lock.

Air whooshed through the vents, undoubtedly carrying odorless gas designed to kill me. To kill both of us, if Macy wasn't already dying.

I was out of time.

I layered four sections of cotton sheeting over each other, wrapping the resulting makeshift mask over my mouth and nose and tying it as tightly as possible at the back of my head.

I had to hope there were too many people who the Collective viewed as assets on the medical level to indiscriminately flood the halls with gas. Not until everyone was evacuated, at least. I had to hope that whoever was overseeing security didn't decide to immediately gas the other four. Or that not all of them were trapped in their rooms yet.

I dropped to the floor, crawling back toward Macy and the bed. Putting the air vents at the top of the walls was practical for camera angles, but the gas would take time to settle.

Of course, they thought they had me trapped.

I grabbed the IV stand and Macy's arm. Keeping low, I dragged the stand and the healer back to the door. She was still alive. Good. I propped her up against the wall under the electronic locking mechanism. Quickly unscrewing the wheeled base of the IV stand, I snapped the pole in half. The metal twisted, then finally tore.

Using its razor-sharp edges, I slashed Macy's wrists.

She didn't have enough strength to cry out.

Blood spurted.

My eyes started stinging from whatever gas they were pumping into the room.

I soaked the last section of sheeting in Macy's blood, pressing the sopping rag against the door lock's palm reader. I grabbed Macy's hand and held it in place, my hand pinning hers.

Then I pushed all the magic I had at my disposal through Macy's hand—and therefore through the residual magic contained in Macy's blood. Attempting to perform hasty, completely unsophisticated blood magic.

The lock sparked, then shorted out.

The door clicked but didn't open.

I hadn't expected it to. Its electronic innards would have been compromised by the pulse of magic, though.

But I was starting to get lightheaded. Dizzy.

I dropped Macy. She slumped, sliding sideways down the wall to sprawl on the tile.

Dead.

But latent empathy or not, I couldn't bring myself to feel sorry about murdering the healer before she'd managed to finish me. Proper kill order or otherwise.

I moved to the door, bringing the two pieces of the IV stand with me. I forced the end of one past the edge of the door and heaved. I stumbled, falling to my knees. But the door opened a smidge. Staying down, I wedged the piece of the stand farther into the door, getting it open about an inch. Then I worked the second piece in, pulling them in opposite directions to create leverage.

I forced the door open about two inches. I pressed my swaddled face into the gap to breathe the air from the hall in gulps and gasps. Then, holding my breath, I attacked the door again, wrenching it open just far enough that I could squeeze through it.

I crawled out into the corridor, coughing and retching.

Keeping low and dragging one of the pieces of the IV stand with me, I slipped into the empty, dark room across the hall.

I pressed my back up against the wall just inside the open door, then wedged the IV stand in the door track so they couldn't lock me in remotely. I tugged the sheeting away from my mouth, leaving it hanging around my neck as I glanced around for water. A bathroom stood to my far left.

The silent alarm went off. The digital station over my head began flashing evacuation orders, indicating which elevators and stairwells would remain open. A ten-minute countdown took over the screen.

"Took you long enough," I whispered, coughing. "Sloppy, sloppy."

A well-armed tactical team would already be on their way. Unless the Collective wanted to sacrifice more employees. But I had time to get a drink of water.

Using the wall for support, I gained my feet, then made it to the bathroom.

THE MEDICAL FACILITIES WERE ON LEVEL TWO OF the compound, two floors underground. Our rooms were below that on the third level, sharing space with the common areas—lounge, cafeteria, gym—and the employee wing. But there was only one way to access the section of level three where the Five had lived since we were preteens. Only one elevator, one stairwell. Both would be locked, and I didn't want to rely on magic I had no actual ability to perform to get me through them.

If I was being honest with myself, it was next to a miracle that I'd gotten out of the room with a completely inept application of blood magic in the first place. Magic worked oddly, especially around anything electronic. At a guess, I had been successful only because Macy had already been tied to the locking mechanism. She had touched it dozens upon dozens of times previously.

The team dispatched to intercept me would expect me to go up, not down. Same with the security detail tracking me through the cameras. They would expect me to try to escape, not to free the others. Short-term, reactionary thinking. But I couldn't make it out of the compound without the other four. And even if I did, I'd be hunted down within days, if not hours. The compound was situated smack in the middle of a South American highland rainforest. I had nowhere to go. For most of our early years, our handlers had tried to keep the actual location of the compound a secret from the Five. Doing so had forced them to jump through many a magical hoop. Unfortunately, they couldn't breed us for what they needed us for without making us smart. Tactical, rational choices had to be made on the fly. And if separated or compromised while on a mission, we had to be able to fend for ourselves. We needed to be able to blend in, to not draw unwanted attention.

As such, we were educated relatively normally to some extent, though lessons about the world at large were always secondary to our physical and magical conditioning. Each of us knew how to operate multiple types of vehicles, but only Fish displayed a talent for mechanics and had been given further training. None of us knew how to cook, or even really how to clean. But Zans could drop a magical virus into a computer and strip it of anything the Collective wanted to get their hands on. We were taught math, reading, writing, logic. No history or music, though. None of the arts. Our access to books of any kind and to mass media was severely limited. All our education had a purpose.

At Christmas, though, the employees used to hold a party in the cafeteria and lounge. And when the ongoing absence of the Five from the festivities had gotten too noticeable, we'd been tasked to attend, like it was a mission. During the last party, I watched my first holiday movie, ate gingerbread, and drank eggnog. The creamy drink had tasted terrible, but I'd loved the cookies and the movie, *Die Hard*.

There were so many other things that we only knew existed because Bee started teaching herself about them. Then she started teaching us, through images and thoughts plucked from the minds of those around us. Because no matter how many charms the employees of the compound wore, keeping a telepath of Bee's power out of their heads was nearly impossible.

The Collective had tried to keep us ignorant in so many aspects of our lives. Perhaps because it fostered a dependence on them? A dependence on each other? Maybe they wanted to make us afraid to even think about leaving. But where would we go? And why would we even think about doing so?

Unless, of course, we were fleeing an attempt on our lives.

Even the team members we worked with most closely didn't know the compound's exact location. Most of them were teleported in and out—and they were all well paid to not ask questions. Our contact with the overseer and the few people local to the compound was severely limited. But unfortunately for the Collective's obsessive need to keep us cloistered, once the Five started to be sent out on active missions, group teleportation from the compound to another secure facility wasn't always an option. Planes and other transportation had to be used. And coastlines and main roads could be compared with maps, which we'd been taught to read because that was knowledge we needed for clandestine extractions.

Things like common accents, currency, and clothing could be assessed, further narrowing down where the Collective's main base of operations was situated. Adding in the lack of seasonal change to light and the length of the day, we figured out eventually that the compound was situated in the mountains of northern Peru. But given my current situation—naked, without weapons, and still healing—knowing my general location didn't help me. Fleeing through the rainforest, even if I did manage to source some clothing and food before I went, wasn't a great option.

At least not alone.

Repeatedly rinsing my nose and mouth cleared them of the gas as much as possible—though I couldn't do anything about whatever had made it into my bloodstream. When I was done, I ignored the evacuation plan on the digital reader at the door. Stepping out into the empty corridor, I headed in the opposite direction. Keeping to the side of the hall, my bare feet were practically silent on the tile underfoot. I tried to dash between camera positions, though I could only guess at their actual angles of view. Finding a blind spot was likely impossible, but if I moved quickly enough, I might fool security for a moment.

I felt a brush of magic from up ahead. A single sorcerer by its tenor. I dashed forward again, pressing myself back against the wall near the next doorway.

A blond sorcerer exited that doorway. His head was down as he concentrated on stuffing a laptop into his satchel. Taking computers or other devices capable of digital storage from the compound was strictly monitored.

Not that the sorcerer would make it to the checkpoint.

I slipped up behind him, wishing he was taller than me so that I might have had the option to use him to physically mask my presence. I grabbed him at the back of his neck. Before he could react, I was already pulling his magic from him. Confusion, then dismay, flashed through me. His emotions, not mine.

The sorcerer's power flowed up my arm and across my chest. I coated myself in it, rather than absorbing it. Hoping to form a loop between us, hoping to confuse the cameras long enough to get through the next set of doors.

"Keep walking," I murmured.

He stumbled but kept moving. "What … you?"

He tried to look back at me, but I firmed my grip on his neck, disabusing him of the notion.

We approached the secondary exit to the medical wing. I reached around the sorcerer, taking his badge.

"Lock," I murmured.

He pressed his palm to the reader. The door whooshed open. I let the sorcerer go, instantly absorbing the magic I'd collected from him as I lost contact with his skin. I couldn't drag him with me. He'd slow me down.

The sorcerer stumbled to the side, rubbing his neck. He raked his gaze over me, head to foot, lingering on the scars slashed across my stomach and lower rib cage. "Amp5. I ... never thought I'd see you in person."

"Well," I said, stepping through the door before it slid closed. "It's your lucky day. I suggest you stay on your side of the door."

"Or what? You'll kill me?"

I laughed harshly. "It's me they're trying to kill. Once the level is mostly evacuated, they'll flood whatever corridor I'm in with gas. The doors seal, so you'll survive if you stay behind this one."

I kept walking, instinctively picking out the locations of the cameras up ahead. Though that information was fairly useless to me without a premade obfuscation spell that might have concealed me from view.

The sorcerer jutted his head through the door. "Kill you? That's insane. You are ... you are perfection. Why would they kill you?"

The door slid closed, almost taking the sorcerer's head with it as he stumbled back.

That was the question. Why kill me? No assessments. No rehabilitation. Making an attempt on my life without a proper kill order felt personal. Except I had no relationships, no interactions that could have possibly created any sort of enemy. Especially not an enemy willing to incur the wrath of the Collective in order to wipe me out.

So perhaps whoever had sent Macy after me had no idea what they were triggering.

I reached over my shoulder, pressing my fingers to the blood tattoo on my T2 vertebra. Bee's blood, Bee's magic under my skin.

"Bee," I murmured, trying to get the telepath's attention and hoping she wasn't completely warded. Hoping that she and the others weren't already dead.

The lack of a proper kill order gave me hope that the other four still survived. But whoever was monitoring the situation, whoever was orchestrating it, would figure out my intentions quickly enough. And incapacitating the others—locking them in their rooms, knocking them out—would be a smart response.

"Bee," I murmured. "I'm out."

Nothing.

I continued forward.

Alone.

A CLUSTER OF SORCERERS HAD FORTIFIED THE DOORS to the stairwell ahead—and undoubtedly the entire staircase leading down to the third level. Evidently, I hadn't fooled anyone as to my objective.

A murder of sorcerers. Not a cluster. Bee's presence brushed through my mind. She laughed, quietly deadly.

"Helpful," I muttered, more relieved than annoyed. "Is everyone okay?"

The telepath didn't answer.

I risked a glance down the long straight hall. Looking for possible egresses or anything I could use for shelter. There were none, which I'd already known—it was a straight run of concrete between me and the rest of the Five. But double-checking never hurt.

A red laser sight bloomed on the wall above me. I was crouched down, so the gun-toting tactical team were aiming for where my head should have been. I retreated a couple of steps, running the floor plan in my head. I could backtrack, come at the stairs from one level down. But since they knew where I was going, eliminating the other four while they were trapped in their rooms was no doubt already being discussed.

A botched attempt on my life was one thing. Perhaps the heart attack Macy had planned to induce was supposed to look like a complication from my wounds. But no matter that Zans thought the entire fifth generation was expendable if I died, murdering the others without a traceable kill order was going to be difficult to justify.

Still, time was of the essence.

I recognized three of the magical signatures at the end of the hall. Three of the team gearing up to face off against me. Three people who'd fought at my side for over two years.

The three I'd chosen to not sacrifice on a rooftop in LA.

I stepped out into the hall.

Bee hissed in my mind. *Wait. Wait. I'm trying to make a connection.*

I wasn't waiting.

"Stand down, Amp5!" Mark Calhoun shouted.

I kept walking, one foot in front of the other. Steady but slow. Reaching up, I made a show of plucking the last remaining bandages from my torso and ribs until I was completely naked except for my scars. The magic embedded in the bandages was long faded, but I wanted to show I was unarmed.

Three laser points bloomed on my chest. Undoubtedly two or three more had appeared on my forehead. I didn't need to wonder which was Mark's kill shot. The head. Unquestionably.

I raised my hands to the sides, fingers spread. Then I stepped in a slow circle so they could see my back. Not surrendering. Just showing that there was nowhere I could have been hiding a weapon. Nowhere comfortable, at least.

"Final warning, Amp5," Mark growled.

I couldn't see them yet. They had to be situated behind a camouflage ward that blended with the concrete and the white walls, making the hall appear empty.

"Don't I at least get three warnings, Mark?" I asked.

No answer, but I caught a whisper of movement. Someone shifting their feet. Someone unsure about gunning me down, maybe.

I paused a dozen steps away, feeling magic not my own gathering sluggishly around my spine. Bee's telepathy. She was still fighting through some sort of interference—improved wards on her room, maybe—and trying to use me as an anchor. Plus the tactical team would definitely be holding charms meant to thwart psychic assault.

Of course, such magic didn't always work. Especially against one of the Five.

I raised my hands higher, this time indicating surrender. Calhoun, Don Flynn, and Becca Jackson—the three whose magic I felt ahead of me but still couldn't see—would know that a naked me wasn't as vulnerable as I appeared. They would know that the chance of accidentally brushing their skin against mine was highly likely when every inch of my skin was in play. A thing to be anticipated.

But to the team members I didn't know, I might have appeared to be just a naked, wounded woman offering to surrender.

Calhoun, gun raised and aimed at me, stepped through the ward line at the end of the hall, collapsing the camouflage spell. He was partnered with a male sorcerer I didn't know.

I glanced over his shoulder as he approached, noting the four other members of the tactical team.

Calhoun appeared to be keeping Flynn and Jackson in the second and third lines, respectively. Smart.

"The order was to kill, not capture," the sorcerer with Mark snapped.

Mark didn't answer. But he was close enough now for me to see the tension etched across his face. Hard lines edged his hazel eyes.

"Did you see a certified kill order, Mark?" I asked.

He didn't answer me either.

The sorcerer's fingers tightened on his gun. He double-checked his aim.

Duck. Spin left. Roll. Uppercut. Knox's barked commands echoed through my mind. Bee had made her connection.

The sorcerer flanking Mark pulled the trigger.

I dropped and spun left, feeling the bullet wing my shoulder as the sorcerer tried to adjust his aim on the fly. I rolled forward, stopping at his feet, then straightening and slamming the heel of my right hand under his chin before he could react.

His head snapped back. The force of my blow lifted him about a foot off the ground.

Calhoun spun, his gun only a couple of inches away from the side of my head. Again, he was smart, not touching me with the weapon. I couldn't actually siphon his magic through something he was holding, but it was never a surprise when one of the Five developed a new ability.

The sorcerer fell, slamming down on his back. The other members of the tactical team stepped over and around him, spreading out before me.

"The only possible way you make it through this situation, Calhoun, is by putting a bullet in my brain. Here." I turned my head so that I could look Mark directly in the eye. "Let's make it easier. Impossible to miss. As long as your gun doesn't backfire."

"My gun never backfires." His tone was tense but determined.

"I know."

Bee's magic churned around me, then brushed through the assembled sorcerers. The three unknowns, one still on the ground but shaking his head, muttered disconcertedly.

Calhoun, Flynn, and Jackson aren't protected against me, Socks.

I smiled at Mark, tightlipped. Acknowledging in silence that I understood he and the others had made a deliberate choice when they'd been tasked to stand against the Five. Against me.

Calhoun grimaced. Then with a quick shift of his gun, he put bullets in the heads of the three new team members. The two still standing fell before any of them could react.

Three people died because my team was still loyal to me. Murdered to save my life. The toll on my soul was endless, even if I wasn't the one pulling the trigger.

"Flank Amp5," Calhoun barked.

Flynn and Jackson stepped back, briefly pressing their shoulders to mine.

"Some clothing might have been a good idea, Amp5." Becca Jackson flashed her teeth at me, the gleam of her sorcerer magic edging her eyes. "You look a little chilly."

Taking point, Calhoun stepped over the fallen, gun raised. Together, we stepped over the inactive ward, crossing into the stairwell. The door was wedged open. Once there, Jackson removed her gloves, reached over and tore the screen off the digital reader. She reached inside, ripping through the innards of the tech, gathering it all in one hand. Then with an intense pulse of her magic, she shorted out the system. In this section, at least.

A demolitions expert at work.

Calhoun glanced over at me. "We'll get you out of the building. There are emergency vehicles parked about five klicks east of the compound." He glanced over at Flynn.

The weapons specialist nodded. "My first year here, I had to drive out and check on them once a week, making sure they were in operating condition, keeping the supply depot stocked. Scut work. Until I got assigned to you, Socks. I can get you there."

"No," I said.

Calhoun shoved his face in mine. "You will listen to me, Amp5. I will get you out of here. And then we'll be even."

I laughed quietly as I reached up to touch his face. Allowing myself the momentary contact and the hint of his anger and frustration that came with it. His stubble was rough under my fingertips. "We were already even, Mark. But they'll kill the others if I leave without them."

"They're not going to destroy their entire program."

"Program?" I asked mockingly.

"Yes," he spat. "You think we're idiots? We get what's going on here, with you five. No names, the separate quarters. You think we haven't noticed that you never set foot out of the compound without an armed guard?"

"Sometimes that guard is us," Becca Jackson said. "And we ain't there to stop someone from getting to you. We're there so you don't get away. Even soldiers can read between the lines."

"Does anyone have an extra gun?" I asked.

Don Flynn pressed a handgun into my hand. The magic coating it tickled against my skin. "It's warded against backfire. Not certain how it'll stand up to your magic, though."

"Thank you." I met Mark's steady gaze. "Thank you. I'll meet you at the off-site depot."

"You're not going without us," Calhoun said.

"This isn't your fight. You don't want to witness this part. Tek5 is going to bring it all down. You don't want to get caught in the backlash of her vengeance."

"Fine. We'll get the others out and leave you to your rampage."

"And then we'll be even?" I asked teasingly.

A rare smile ghosted across Mark's face, gone before I'd fully registered it. Then he turned his back on me, heading for the stairs.

I followed. I couldn't force them to leave ahead of me. But I also had no way of guaranteeing their safety. That was how it had always been between us, how it would always be if they stayed with me.

The steps I'd already been forced to take, along with Zans's desire for revenge, ensured that I'd be hunted for the rest of my life—if I made it out of the compound alive. So I was going to make it worth it.

FIVE

TUCKED BETWEEN THE LAST THREE REMAINING members of my extraction team, I made my way down the concrete stairs. Becca Jackson continued to short out cameras and digital displays as we passed, but after we made it into the airlock at the third level, neither Calhoun's badge nor the one I'd stolen from the sorcerer on the medical level would open the second set of doors. The only doors that led to the quarters of the Five.

Jackson set to work on the locking mechanism, trying to access and reprogram it, rather than short it out. I pressed my ear to the sealed door, visualizing the long hall that lay behind it. White-painted concrete walls and floors. Six steel doors—one for each of us, and a spare. Why there were six rooms for the five of us, we'd never known.

My guess had always been that there were once plans for us to be the Six, not just five. Though what magic the sixth of our generation would have wielded, I couldn't even guess.

The other four could have been dying just on the other side of the airlock. Separated from each other, unable to fully access their magic, and gassed … poisoned … murdered … as they tried to break out of their rooms. Because of me.

I'd always been the responsible one, the rational one. Trained to lead, to inspire confidence and commitment. Designed at a cellular level through to conception and birth to be the epicenter, the core … the heart of the Five.

I stepped back from the door, giving the tech and demolitions specialist space to work. Jackson didn't need me screwing up her process with any wild magic called forth by an irrational emotional response.

Mark Calhoun was watching me. I cut my gaze toward him then looked deliberately away. He turned his focus to the door behind us, covering our rear.

The airlock door sighed, then shifted open an inch. I surged forward. Bracing my left palm on the frame, I attempted to wrench the door farther open with my right. Pressing against me, Calhoun and Flynn grabbed the door below and above me. Between the three of us, we muscled it open.

The hall was dark.

It was never dark.

A terrible pit yawned open in my stomach.

"Masks," Mark snapped, placing a tiny breathing apparatus over his mouth and nose. The other two mimicked him, placing masks on their faces as well.

I strode forward, pausing before the first door to the right. Bee's door. Jackson pressed a spare mask into my hand. I took it but didn't put it on. Then she mumbled a single word as she tossed a trio of small stones down the hall. Three miniature spotlights bloomed from each stone, leaving strange pits of shadow sporadically along the walls.

"Nul5?" Calhoun asked. "Amp5, which door leads to the nullifier?"

I shook my head, realizing that I'd been oddly frozen in place. Getting Fish out first made perfect sense. Once freed, he and Jackson could work separately to free the others.

The airlock door shuddered, then slid back into place behind me.

"Shit," Becca muttered. "That was fast. They've got the new whiz kid in the booth."

I didn't know who she was talking about, but I inferred that the appearance of new staff since the roof incident in LA hadn't been limited to just the medical wing.

"Socks!" Mark snapped. "Nul5?"

"Last door on the right."

Jackson surged forward, racing down the corridor and practically attacking the locking mechanism at the side of the far door. Calhoun and Flynn covered the airlock door.

The hall dead-ended. And I knew from experience that there were triple-thick, magic-and-steel-lined walls between each of the rooms. Our handlers were careful about keeping us separated, or at least maintaining their ability to separate us. But they'd been underestimating our capacity to foil their restraints since we were all in our early teens. Though whenever any of us had managed to sneak out of our rooms and into Fish's, they would eventually figure out a new way to thwart us from doing so again for weeks or months at a time.

I brushed the screen next to Bee's door, attempting to trigger the interior camera. The tech didn't obey my touch.

A slight breeze stirred my hair. It was long enough now to tickle my eyelashes when I looked up. The sensation was so novel that I had actually lifted my face to it before I realized they'd switched on the gas.

I placed the mask Jackson had given me over my mouth and nose, banging on Bee's door even though I knew it was too thick for her to hear me. Magic stirred lazily through the second-highest blood tattoo on my spine.

Socks? You here?

"I am. I'm here, Bee. Tell the others."

The connection is spotty.

"Are they gassing you, Bee? Bee?"

She didn't answer.

Jackson got Nul5's door partially open. Fish wrenched it the rest of the way, then practically shoved Becca aside as he charged from his room. His gaze met mine—furious but under control—as Jackson shoved a breathing apparatus into his hand. He nodded as he put it on, then stepped across the hall, laying his hand across the locking mechanism for Tek5's door.

Fish was wearing his armor but wasn't carrying any weapons. We weren't allowed weapons on level three or in our rooms. But then, we were the weapons. I still wanted to collect my blades, though. And some sort of clothing would be a good idea.

I already had the perfect outfit in mind.

The mask was keeping my lungs clear, but my eyes were starting to sting from whatever they were pumping into the hall. Nul5 was still focused on Zans's door, his magic pulsing along the hall. The lock mechanism sparked, then died.

"Clear!" he shouted, moving to the side of the door. His command reverberated through my mind, helped along by Bee.

The door to Tek5's room bulged out, then buckled inwardly. It tore loose from the frame, crumpling in on itself until it was a large ball of metal. Zans stepped into the hall, her hand extended forward. She was also dressed in her flexible armor. So they'd had a heads-up. The crumpled door moved with Zans, just a step ahead.

"Show-off," Fish groused.

Cla5's door slid open. Jackson whooped.

"Down in front!" Zans shouted. She launched the twisted ball of steel down the corridor. It picked up speed, zooming toward the airlock door.

Calhoun and Flynn spun out of the way, shields of magic snapping up around them.

The crumpled door hit the airlock dead center. Zans continued to stride forward, coughing from the gas she'd inhaled. She battered the airlock over and over. It dented, then crumpled, then tore away from its frame.

Fish darted into Knox's room, exiting with Cla5 over his shoulder.

I cried out before I could stop myself, lunging forward as Nul5 laid the clairvoyant on the floor.

Fish moved toward Bee's door before Knox's limp head had even rolled to the side. I dropped to my knees, sliding the last few inches to place my hand on Knox's chest. He wasn't breathing.

Fish tore through the locking mechanism on Bee's door, nullifying magic and electronics alike.

I shoved both hands up Knox's shirt, placing my palms on his chest. He was still dressed in his sweats. The gas had either hit him earlier, or he had less resistance to it than the rest of us. Or he'd been swamped with visions and unable to fully function, locked away from everyone else. I gathered my magic under my hands, readying a huge pulse of amplification. I was hoping to shock his heart with it, hoping to force his magic to revive him. It was intrusive and desperate. But none of us was a healer—a deliberate oversight on the part of the Collective.

Coughing, Fish got Bee's door open, diving through the opening as Jackson moved to my door. Zans had disappeared into the airlock, likely busting her way—our way—up and down the stairwell.

I hit Knox with all the magic I'd gathered, slamming a massive dose of amplification into his chest. He convulsed.

I hit him again.

And again.

His head snapped back with the last blast, body straining upward, teeth and jaw clenched on a scream. The white of his magic flooded through his eyes.

He reared upward, though I tried to hold him down. He grabbed my upper arms hard enough to bruise them, silently screaming.

"I'm sorry," I whispered. "I'm sorry."

A shudder ran through him, and he let me settle him back to the floor.

"Socks," he whispered. "Left, left." But he wasn't talking to me. Well, he was talking to me. Except it was the future me that only he could see in his mind's eye.

"Quit playing around, Amp5," Fish snarled.

I glanced up the hall. Nul5 was carrying Bee from her room.

The telepath was dressed in her armor. So everyone but Knox and me had some extra protection from the magical assault we were about to face. I realized it was possible they'd gassed Knox first, right after I'd gotten out of the med bay. Taking out the clairvoyant before he could see the decision being made to sacrifice the Five made sense.

Jackson got the door to my room open, darting toward the airlock as soon as she did. I disentangled myself from Knox, who was breathing but had closed his eyes. I pressed my breathing apparatus over his nose and mouth as Flynn stepped over to help him up.

"Go ahead of me," I said. "Reconnoiter in the stairwell."

Flynn nodded, moving quickly with Knox propped up on his shoulder.

With the airlock open, the gas was likely diffusing into the stairwell, but I kept low anyway as I stepped into my room. I ignored the armor hanging in my closet, barely giving anything else a second glance. Instead, I crossed to the bed and pulled out the roll of fabric I'd hidden under it. The gift Sasha Piper had given me.

I unrolled the green cotton-and-spandex sundress, quickly tugging it on over my head. It fell to a few inches above my knees.

It felt like freedom.

My eyes were watering as I pulled on panties. I grabbed socks and my tactical boots but didn't linger to put them on.

I had no other personal possessions to take with me.

And even if I had, I would have gladly left every single other thing behind.

THE OTHERS WERE CLUSTERED AT THE LANDING AT level three. Knox and Bee were both on their feet. A hushed but angry argument was in progress between Fish and Calhoun. But everyone turned at my approach, eyeing me as I sat at their collective feet to tug on and lace up my boots.

"What the fuck is that?" Fish snarled.

I ignored him.

"Where is your armor?"

I shrugged. "This is what I'm wearing."

"We trust you to get us out of here, Amp5. We trust you to make this right."

Allowing his anger to wash over me, I cinched my laces tightly, then gained my feet to level a heavy stare at him.

He snapped his mouth shut, looking away from me.

"Out of bounds, Fish," Knox murmured.

"I got that, thanks."

"Calhoun, Flynn, and Jackson are heading straight up and out," I said. "The five of us will be following Zans down to the bottom. Level five. We'll back her mission, then retreat."

Calhoun was already shaking his head. A slow grin spread over Fish's face. This plan was obviously what they'd been fighting about.

"Jackson, do you have any extra respirators?"

"One more." Jackson handed that last mask to Zans. "But the magic threaded through the filter will probably only last another twenty or thirty minutes."

"If we aren't out in thirty minutes," I said, "we're already dead."

Zans spun away with a laugh, heading down the stairs with Fish right behind her.

Calhoun opened his mouth to protest.

"Wait," I said, interrupting him. "Bee? Knox? Heading out with the rest of the team, readying our passage ... if you feel..."

Knox gave me a withering look, turning away to head down the stairs. Bee snorted, crossing her arms.

"I'd like you to reconsider," Mark said quietly.

Jackson and Flynn stepped away.

I eyed the sandy-haired sorcerer. Then I offered him a tight-lipped smile. "I don't regret one minute of being in your bed, Mark."

Bee exhaled, surprised. Then she started coughing, waving me off when I glanced at her in concern.

"Come with me, then," Mark said. "Forget this folly of making the Collective pay."

"I owe them this. The others."

"You don't. You've ... your whole life has already been theirs. Choose your next steps unhindered."

I smiled more genuinely. "I am. I already did. Thank you."

"Then we're coming with you."

"You'll slow us down. We'll worry about accidentally hurting you. And when you die … it will hurt me."

"There's a chance I'm about to die just trying to get out of the building."

I nodded, then I glanced up the stairs to see Jackson and Flynn watching us. "Thank you. It's been … it would all have been a lot harder … all of it … without you."

They nodded in unison.

Then because that was what always happened in every action movie I'd ever seen—all five of them—I pressed a kiss to Mark's lips.

He brushed his fingers through my hair—gifting me with another completely novel sensation—and kissed me back.

"Don't wait for me," I said. "If I'm not right behind you, I'm not coming."

I turned away before he could respond, heading down the stairs with Bee on my heels. I knew Calhoun would get Flynn and Jackson out. He was their commanding officer, and that was more important than one night with me. As it should be.

And what Zans and Fish were about to do would ensure that the Collective would be in disarray long enough that Calhoun, Flynn, and Jackson's involvement in our rebellion would be incidental.

Was it good? With Mark? Better than Fish?

I nodded, answering Bee in my head, not out loud. *Different.*

She made a thoughtful noise, then we found the others waiting for us one level down.

"Weapons cache next," I said.

"Already ahead of you, Socks," Zans said, flicking her fingers toward the door to the corridor.

It crumpled under the assault of her magic, then blew inward.

I swallowed, my throat suddenly tight. "Remember they're people. Just employees."

The four of them turned to look at me as one, magic boiling around them. Deadly and fierce, ready to be released. Completely unfettered.

"Anyone who hasn't evacuated already dies," Fish said coolly. "Either they're in our way, or they leave us vulnerable from behind."

Bee, Knox, and Zans nodded.

"It's okay, Socks," Zans said with a sneer. "Fish and I will take the brunt of the murder and destruction. We're better at it."

She walked away.

The others followed.

I hesitated. But only for a breath.

Six

BREAKING OUT OF THE COMPOUND—OR IN THIS case, farther into it—was much easier with Knox and Bee leading the way. Though physically, the clairvoyant and telepath were kept safely tucked behind us. Thankfully, any staff who hadn't already evacuated the fourth level fled before Zans—especially after we busted into the weapons cache and she got her hands on a dozen explosive devices especially tuned to her telekinesis.

I had retrieved my black blades from the cache, choosing to strap on the combination shoulder sheath even though it ruined the line of my dress. Fish and Knox both selected shortswords. Bee opted for her katana. And Zans had added three pouches of ball bearings to her arsenal, attaching them to her utility belt.

When we were done, Fish had set a timing device on the explosives Zans begrudgingly consented to leave behind. Once triggered, all the ammunition in the cache would also explode. The walls and ceiling were fortified concrete, but with the door wedged open, it would definitely clear out the level. Or it might possibly take the entire floor with it.

I had ordered a fifteen-minute countdown when we exited the weapons cache and headed for the opposite stairs. And we were making good use of that time. Fish was able to wipe out all the cameras along each of the corridors we passed through with a single pulse of his nullifying power. That power didn't just null magic—even magically fortified electronics didn't stand a chance against it. But with no cameras to follow our progress across level four, whoever was attempting to thwart our rampage was actively pumping gas into every hallway. Our masks were going to fail before we got anywhere near the exterior doors on the main aboveground level at the rate we were going. Because we needed to go down before we went up.

None of us had ever set foot on level five. Not while conscious, anyway. But I was headed there now without hesitation, with Bee and Knox at my heels, eager to get away from the gas that felt like it was melting any and all of my exposed skin. The Collective—or whoever was currently making onsite decisions for the Collective—would be careful with level five. Protective.

Level five was where it had all begun.

Level five might be where it all ended.

THE CORRIDOR AT THE BASE OF THE STAIRS WAS deeply shadowed beyond the airlock door. Security had cut the power, either in an attempt to slow us down or as an automated procedure during evacuation. But various bluish lights were seeping into the corridor from open doors and interior windows, so level five either had a separate electrical panel from the rest of the compound or was running backup generators.

I paused, surveying the corridor while giving Zans and Fish time to catch up to us. Bee and Knox stood as close to me as they could without touching me.

"They're gathering upstairs," Bee murmured, her voice remote. "Dozens. At least as far as I can pick up through the layers of shielding."

"They'll be wearing every charm they have," I said. "And by the time we get above ground, they'll all be activated. Hannigan had some of your hair in what I'd swear was a witch charm. A casting that I would have thought was outside his sorcerer abilities. For all we know, the Collective has your hair stored every time it's clipped. Any time any of us are clipped."

Bee's lips compressed. Only our most recently clipped hair would hold enough magic to target us. Such residual power faded once removed. And that meant Hannigan's charm had either been a recent acquisition—or was repeatedly renewed.

"Anyone on this level?" I asked.

"Feedback midway along." That was an indication that someone might be blocking her telepathy.

"Knox?" I whispered. "Got anything for us?"

"We need to move," the clairvoyant said. "And keep moving. But nothing is going to kill us in the next five minutes that I can see."

Fish barreled down the stairs, shouldered past me, and pressed his hand to the lock. I felt Zans stop close behind me. The door clicked but didn't open.

An intense wave of magic brushed by me, ripping the door from the frame and throwing it halfway down the long hall.

Fish glanced back at Zans. "You might want to hold something in reserve."

She shrugged. "Why? I've got Socks to amplify me when I need it. Besides, we're about to blow up the building. I won't even tap my reserves in the next…"—she glanced at the digital watch on her wrist—"…ten minutes."

Nul5 shook his head. Then he stepped forward, raising his hands.

Zans pushed past me, placing her hand on his shoulder. "Not yet."

"We need to knock out the cameras," I murmured.

"Let them watch. They won't risk gassing this section."

Apparently, Zans knew something I didn't. I glanced at Knox. He shook his head, also in the dark.

Tek5 strode forward, breaking protocol by taking point. She paused to glance into the first couple of rooms off the hall.

I followed, relying on Knox and Bee to alert me to anything I couldn't see or feel on my own.

Zans increased her pace to a jog, glancing through doorways. Then with a triumphant cry, she darted left through a windowed door midway along the hall.

I nodded to Fish. He took off after her.

Moving methodically, I glanced into the first room to my right. It was office space of some sort, with more rooms branching off it. Medical charts and other things I had no context to understand or enough light to decipher lined the walls.

The first room on the left was an examination room, with a bathroom beyond.

I continued along the hall, steadily assessing each doorway for hazards and targets. I found none.

Then I came to the lab situated across the hall from the door through which Zans and Fish had disappeared. I paused, staring through the glass door and windows, processing what I was seeing.

Lab equipment, stainless steel counters, glass-fronted fridges.

"Oh, God," Bee whispered. "Oh my God … are those … are those…?" She grabbed Knox's arm.

A series of cylindrical aquariums stood on the far side of the lab. Except the glass tanks weren't holding fish.

Without thinking, I pushed the door. It opened with a whoosh of air. A low hum of electricity emanated from the refrigerators and other containment devices, though the room wasn't lit. I took three steps into the lab before I managed to gain control of myself and my reaction to what I was seeing.

"Fetuses," Knox whispered behind me, finishing Bee's unspoken thought.

Yes. Fetuses in various states of development were suspended in liquid. Dozens and dozens of them. Beyond those glass cases were refrigerators filled with test tubes. I stepped forward until I could read the labels on the middle shelves—Amp5, Nul5, Tek5, Cla5, and Tel5.

Bee moaned, pointing one shelf higher. More test tubes, these ones labeled exactly the same except with a number six in place of the five. The sixth generation.

I went numb. All my emotions shut right down, as often happened in the middle of a battle. I systematically catalogued the tubes on the remaining shelves. Based on the labels, they contained genetic material.

"This is where they cooked us up," Knox said hollowly.

"You already knew that," I said, turning away and ignoring the glimpse I caught of the room through the door to my right.

It was filled with beds. Beds that at some point might have held our surrogate mothers. A room in which I might have stolen my secondary magic, claiming the power of empathy during the trauma of birth. And killing the woman who'd carried me under her skin, who'd fed me with her blood and magic.

That much of my birth, I had pieced together. But I knew those details only because various handlers had related the story over and over again. "To control me," I whispered through numb lips. "To subdue me. To make me afraid of my own power."

Knox and Bee stepped in front of me, filling my line of sight and calling my attention, my focus, back to the room, to the situation.

"We need to move," I said.

But I didn't.

"We should move," I said again.

Knox nodded, then he stepped back and opened each refrigerator door.

"Zans will take care of that," Bee murmured.

"This will make certain that nothing survives."

I strode toward the exit, stepping into the hall and quickly crossing into the room that had been Zans's primary focus.

Banks of hard drives and various tech lined all the walls of the large room. A massive workstation with a long desk filled with monitors and keyboards sat at the very center. A chair was overturned. A cup of coffee had spilled and pooled across the floor. Someone had left in a hurry.

Zans's fingers were flying over the keyboard at the center of the desk. Her attention was fixated on data streaming across the monitor. "Wait ... wait..."

"We're out of time." Fish was moving from bank to bank of hard drives, placing his hands on each in turn and frying anything electronic with focused pulses of his magic.

"We're going," I said coolly, turning away before I'd even fully entered the room.

Fish glanced at me, nodding.

Zans glanced at her watch to check the count-down timer in the weapons cache. "We've still got eight minutes."

"To clear the building," I snapped.

She laughed brittlely. "We'll survive."

"Fish," I said.

Obeying my call without question, he immediately crossed to me.

"Don't you dare, Socks!" Zans shouted, frantically typing on the keyboard.

I placed my hand on Nul5's back over his armor, knowing that the tattoo of my blood lay just underneath. A tattoo that allowed my amplifier power to affect the nullifier when all other magic rolled off him.

"You owe me, Amp5!" Zans shrieked.

"I don't, actually," I said. Then I started pumping my power into Fish.

He gasped, arching up and forward, then spread his arms.

Zans lunged for a nearby tower, tearing loose what appeared to be a series of portable hard drives. I had no idea where she would have gotten anything that could have been used to transport data.

"Three…" I said.

Zans screamed, pulling another drive, then another.

"Two…"

She turned to glare at me, baring her teeth in a snarl of utter loathing.

"One."

Zans leaped toward the door, tearing past us and into the hall.

Fish let loose with everything he had and everything I'd pumped into him. In a flash, his magic swamped the entire room, wiping every device and drive. Monitors exploded. Sparks flew. The bank of drives that Zans had been tearing apart caught fire.

I dropped my hand from Fish's back, turning into the hall and catching his shudder in my peripheral vision. He shuddered just like that when he orgasmed. Releasing that much magic, having my magic flowing through him unfettered, had to feel better than any tumble he'd ever enjoyed. Though since he was the only one that any of the Five could sleep with without magical repercussions, he had way more experience with that than I did. So I might not have enough context to form an opinion.

Zans was sprawled on the floor in the corridor. I stepped over her, heading toward the door at the far end.

"You're a stuck-up bitch," she snarled after me.

I didn't bother to look back. "You said you were going to take it down, Tek5. Time to step up and prove your word."

She scrambled to her feet, jogging after me. "Give me a bump, then."

I paused before the airlock at the base of the stairwell, having not bothered to open any doors or even glance through the windows between me and the stairs. I didn't want to know what else was housed on this level. I never wanted to know.

Fish, Bee, and Knox joined us.

Zans pressed the drives she'd collected into Fish's hands. "I need you to ward these."

"It might not hold with the amount of magic we're about to throw around."

"Please," she begged.

He nodded, tucking the drives into various pockets on his armor, then stepped over to open the airlock at our backs. It was only smart to have an egress before Zans and I got started.

Fish got the door open, stepping through it. Bee and Knox followed.

I shifted behind Zans, placing my hand on the back of her neck, skin to skin. She flung out her hands before her, launching three tiny explosive devices from each, then giving them a push with her power.

I took everything she had and amplified it. I pumped her full of my power, doubling the strength of her own magic. Tripling it.

That magic streamed from her. The devices exploded at the other end of the hall, taking out walls, doors, and windows. Fire raged toward us—and Zans fueled it, tearing through anything that hadn't been touched by the first explosion with her telekinesis. The corridor warped with magic, concrete and metal twisting, shredding.

"Fuck…" Fish snarled, stepping up beside me just in time to cast a countering wave of magic, creating a nullifying shield between us and the destruction Zans had wrought. "Be more careful next time."

"We need to go," Knox murmured. "Now. They're about to hit the weapons cache."

Zans cackled. "And find our little surprise."

"Exactly."

Bee, Knox, and Zans darted for the stairs.

Then I heard the cry.

It was just a whisper. A sound of mewling pain. I tracked it. It was coming through the closed door to my immediate right.

My heart began beating wildly. Something was alive beyond that door. And dying.

Ignoring the inferno raging behind the ward Nul5 was still holding in place, I spun toward the door.

"Leave it," Fish grunted. He had clearly heard it too.

I ignored him. The door was intersected by Fish's magic about three-quarters of the way across. But though the handle was on my side of the ward Fish was holding, the hinges weren't.

"We have to go," Knox shouted behind me.

"Let me pass, Fish,"

With a pained grunt, Nul5 shoved his magic toward the inferno, pushing it back just enough to clear the doorway.

I grasped the handle, searing my skin—the heat of the fire was already seeping through the walls. As I shoved the door open, the terrible stench of charred flesh assaulted my senses. I gagged, stepping into the room that lay beyond.

Over half of it was already destroyed. Fire was raging, smoke filling the air. Overturned cages were everywhere. As with the fetuses and the genetic material on this level, the Collective had apparently also been experimenting on animals, though to what end, I didn't know.

My eyes watered. The heat baked my skin.

Something whimpered again, drawing my attention to the far right corner of the room. A pile of dark-furred creatures had clustered under a workstation, having broken out of their cages. But they'd been unable to get out of the room.

A terrible sob was wrenched from me. I threw myself to my knees. I could barely see through the smoke and heat, but I could feel a faint hum of magic. That had to mean that one of the creatures was still alive.

"Socks! Socks!" Knox was screaming, pushing into the room behind me.

Magic whispered around me. Fish was trying to shift his ward to give me some cover.

I reached into the furry, still-warm pile of bodies. Gently lifting one, then another to the side, I searched, searched, searched for the tiny sliver of magic I could still feel. But they were dead.

They were all dead.

Because of me.

Again and again, all I did was take and destroy.

I was sobbing now, crying like I'd never cried in my life.

Bee was there, grabbing my arm, attempting to pull me away. I fought her off, still carefully digging through the tiny furry corpses. I could feel a spark of magic. I would have sworn I could feel it.

More hands grabbed me, Zans working with Bee now. I knocked them back with a nasty pulse of my magic. That was what they got for touching my skin.

Then Knox was crouching next to me, reaching past me and pressing a small warm body into my hands. Sharp teeth bit me. Then the little creature Knox had found suckled at the wound it had created.

The three of them dragged me from the room, back into the stairwell. My skin had blistered painfully, tears streaming down my face. I coughed and coughed.

Something exploded above us.

The other four hunkered around me. Nul5 tightened the ward he was still holding so that it covered us tightly.

The building shook.

I wiped my face. Then I looked down at the furry creature I'd rescued.

It was a blue-furred puppy with viciously sharp teeth. And a tiny mane of tentacles that hummed with magic.

So, not just a dog.

The puppy blinked red-orbed eyes at me—clearly marking it as some sort of demon hybrid. Then it wrapped one of its tentacles around my thumb.

"Bred to track us," Zans said.

"How do you know?" I asked.

She nodded toward Fish, who'd laid out her hard drives before him on the concrete floor. He was systematically warding them. "It's on one of those. One of their experiments. If I can still retrieve the data."

"Then we kill it," Fish said.

I looked at him steadily. Then I smiled, letting him know I'd murder him, or any of them, before I'd allow them to kill the innocent creature in my hands. A creature that hadn't asked to become what it was. Just as we five had been given no choice.

Everyone else in the compound, anyone else working for the Collective, had made the decisions that had shaped all our lives, wooed by money and the accumulation of power. And I would kill any of them who stood between me and saving the others. But the puppy was untarnished.

Fish grimaced. "You could have just said no. Put it in Zans's backpack, then. You need your hands free."

"No."

Another explosion rocked the compound. Then another. We all paused, looking up at the stairwell. It held.

Zans shucked off her pack, retrieving the last of the explosive devices from it and clipping them to her belt. She shoved the empty pack at me.

I passed the demon puppy to Knox, touching the back of his hands lightly. "Thank you."

He nodded. The skin on the left side of his face was a deep pink.

I could only imagine how much worse I looked. I got the backpack on frontways, cinching it as tightly as I could over my chest. I couldn't wear it on my back without it interfering with my blades. Knox tucked the demon puppy in the bag, but it started to whine when he zipped it up.

Fish locked his gaze to me. "You are absolutely, mind-bogglingly ridiculous."

Zans snorted.

I unzipped the pack, just enough that the demon puppy could stick its nose out. "We aren't going to die because I stopped to rescue a dog. We're going to die because of you and Zans, and your little revenge side project."

Tension rippled through Fish's face, but he didn't deny my assessment. Zans looked away.

I wasn't stupid.

"So when we do die, it'll be on your heads," I said coolly. "Pray you go first. Because if your screwing around with data collection gets Bee or Knox killed, I'll murder you both myself."

Neither of them answered me. But then, what could they have said?

I could kill them. That had never been in question.

"Let's move." I stood up.

Fish dropped his shield. Nothing fell on our heads.

I headed for the stairs. "They'll come at us with everything now."

The four of them gathered around me without question. We headed up.

Fish was in front, holding a mobile shield. Me behind him. Bee and Knox on either side of me. Zans at the rear. If we were attacked, Knox and Bee would drop back, and Zans would step up beside Fish where I could amplify both of them at the same time.

Only five levels to go.

Seven

"HOLD," KNOX WHISPERED.

We paused halfway up the northeast stairs that led to level two, waiting, watching as Cla5's magic ringed his light-gray eyes, then faded.

He shook his head grimly. "This isn't going to be good."

"Beyond our control?" I asked.

He nodded.

Nul5 dropped his shield and my ears popped. Then he snapped it back into place, taking a moment to reinforce it. Zans shifted so she was ahead of me. Then she and Fish, shoulder to shoulder, started climbing again.

"Oh," Bee whispered beside me. "Flynn's dying."

My foot slipped on the edge of a step. I compensated, brushing away the pinch of dread trying to drill into my stomach.

Knox nodded curtly, confirming that the pending death of my teammate was what he'd already deemed unchangeable. He had seen more than that, of course. But Knox kept what he saw to himself more often than not. After twenty-one years, he had figured out what battles were worth fighting. Not that he could control what any of us chose to do when faced with a challenge he had already deemed impossible.

Zans pushed past the rest of us and onto the landing first. Her dark-eyed gaze fell on something in the far corner. She glanced back at me as Fish brushed by her to secure the door leading to the second-level corridor. I couldn't read the telekinetic's expression, though her battle stare usually alternated between stoic and jovial.

She wasn't feeling playful now.

I stepped past her.

Flynn was tucked into the corner by the door, facing the upper stairs. His face was ashen, eyes closed.

I stumbled again, but managed the five steps necessary to kneel by his side. He looked dead already, blood staining his chin, neck, and chest. His hands were cupped at his waist.

Jackson had slashed an X across his chest with her rune-marked red tape. Which didn't make any sense. She wasn't a healer.

"Socks," Flynn said, choking up blood. "Been waiting for you." He opened his eyes. They were rimmed with blood and boiling with his unleashed magic.

Pain ricocheted through my stomach that had nothing to do with my wounds. I clamped down on it.

"Yeah," Flynn gurgled. "It was a hell of a curse. Shredded our shields. I took the brunt of it, so ... no worries for Becca or Mark."

I reached for him, brushing my fingers against his cheeks.

He sighed. "No, Socks. I'm gone. I've been holding on for you." His gaze flicked to various points over my head, then settled on Zans over my right shoulder. "You'll only waste your magic on me. I was dead the second the curse hit me. But..." He bowed his head, looking down.

He opened his cupped hands. Dark-blue power, teeming with energy, was pooled in his palms. He began to cough, blood flooding out of his mouth. Somehow, he managed to catch most of it in his hands. The magic he'd collected flared and expanded.

Now the rune-marked tape made sense. Flynn was readying his final spell—a sure-to-be potent death curse. Becca had hoped to help him anchor it with the tape, waiting for us, holding. Building on the curse until he was ready to unleash it ... ready to die.

A terrible pain gripped me, tearing through my chest, then forcing its way out through my throat in a ragged sob.

"Hey now, darling," Flynn murmured. "I should have died on our first mission ... Aruba ... do you remember? You stepped in, took that ... curse..."

I remembered the mission, but hadn't known the location. "It was meant for me."

"No, Socks. You never did figure out that part ... we were always there for you, as much as you were there for us…" His voice faded, and he closed his eyes.

I reached for him again, but this time touching him tenderly as I never could have when he was… among the living. But in this half-life, I could reach for his emotions. I could feel his fear and his resolution.

He took a shuddering breath. "Go now," he said. "I need to cast."

"I could—"

"No. Go now, Socks. They've blockaded the stairs, you'll need to cross through… level two. Calhoun and Jackson are right in front of you. Go … go. Don't say goodbye."

I dropped my hand from his cheek, standing and stepping away through the door where Fish held his shield, waiting. Knox and Bee touched the top of Flynn's head, then stepped into the hall.

"Zans," Flynn whispered.

I glanced back to see Tek5 set one knee on the floor and lean over the dying sorcerer.

"I wish…" Flynn coughed up more blood. "I meant to kiss you at the Christmas party. Before it got shut down."

Zans clenched her hands into fists.

I looked away, meeting and holding Fish's inscrutable gaze.

"But … but I knew I wasn't worthy of you … of your … your…"

I shoved myself against Fish's shield, desperately needing to be out of hearing distance.

He grunted, but shifted the magic standing between me and the corridor stretching out before us. Five steps was all it took. Either Flynn had stopped talking, or I couldn't hear his dying declaration anymore. The words weren't meant for my ears anyway.

Magic brushed across my bare collarbone, licking my skin. I glanced down into the backpack, wrapping my hand around the demon puppy as another short tentacle curled up from the mane ringing its neck and brushed against my fingers. Magic followed, scouring Flynn's blood from my hand.

"Paisley," Knox murmured. "Her name is Paisley."

"Okay," I said, not questioning the name or the gender. "Paisley." Knox had named the Five, after all, whether some of us liked his choices or not.

Zans stood abruptly, striding toward us. Her entire body was tensed in fury. That emotion I could pick out easily enough, but I'd never seen the telekinetic wield her anger with such cold disdain.

"Move," she said. "I'll take point. Nul5, we're going to need to be shielded from the back."

Fish opened his mouth to rip her head off—for assuming she could order him to do anything, let alone tell him to do his duty even as he was already doing it.

I shook my head.

He clamped his mouth shut, falling back behind Bee and Knox.

WE WERE ABOUT THREE-QUARTERS OF THE WAY along the corridor when Flynn unleashed his death curse in the northeast stairwell.

By succumbing to death.

Magic slammed against Fish's nullifying field. It actually shoved him forward into Knox and Bee.

The concrete floor rumbled under our feet. Anyone in the path of the spell, whatever team was blocking the northeast stairwell and whoever had hit Flynn with the spell that had killed him, wouldn't be left standing. In fact, based on the light display pulsing across Fish's shield, I doubted whether the stairwell would even be passable.

A sorcerer of Flynn's caliber held a lot of magic in his blood, in his life force. Enough to wipe out many enemies.

But then, if you were willing to die to do so, you could wreak a lot of vengeance.

Waiting for the residual to fade before moving, we all turned to look at Zans.

She was standing a couple of steps ahead, head bowed, hands clenched at her sides.

Flynn's magic faded.

Zans glanced back down the corridor, snarling and laughing at the same time. "I bet that stung them.

And I haven't even gotten started yet." She pinned her dark gaze to me. "Are you with me, Socks?"

She didn't have to ask. Truthfully, she really shouldn't have asked, because there was wild magic embedded in vows—when the words were wielded by those such as us.

"To the end," I said.

"To the end." Knox, Bee, and Fish echoed the words behind me.

Magic shifted around us, then settled. We were already tied. By birth, by blood, and by magic. Those bonds might have been forced upon us, but we had no one else. No reason not to die for each other.

KNOX FELL AT THE ENTRANCE TO THE SOUTHEAST stairwell leading to level one. I felt a thick strand of dark magic brush past my shoulder, just before the clairvoyant shoved himself in front of Bee and took the blood curse aimed at the telepath in the chest.

A named spell. It could have been nothing less to get through Fish's shield.

Meant for Bee.

Designed to kill her.

Which meant that the Collective had more than hair clippings stored elsewhere in the compound. Or someone with forethought had collected what they needed from level five before we destroyed it. They had blood samples, and taken recently. Because once blood was removed from a body, the magic within it faded quickly.

Moreover, for such a spell to get through Fish's nullifying field, there was no doubt that a black witch had just sacrificed a life to fuel it. Maybe even slaughtered one of the tactical team that still stood between us and freedom.

That wasn't going to be good for morale.

Bee shrieked, grabbing for Knox as he staggered back.

"Zans!" I shouted.

Zans grabbed Bee, pulling her away so she couldn't touch Knox—not while the spell was still live, still seeking its ultimate target.

Fish grabbed Knox, lowering the clairvoyant to the concrete floor. The named spell solidified into a black creeping mass, spiderwebbing across Knox's chest. The only reason the clairvoyant was able to step in front of the curse at all was because of the tattoo inked in Bee's blood on his spinal cord.

The curse had to be fulfilled. There wasn't any other way to break it. The named victim had to die.

But … the Five might be able to hold it at bay.

Knox groaned, pained, arching up as the curse dug into his flesh, tasting his magic.

"You could have said something," Fish growled.

"No time," Knox gasped.

I kneeled beside the clairvoyant, reaching for Fish's hand, for his permission. Nul5 nodded, hovering his hand over the curse on Knox's chest, palm down.

I placed my hand on top of his, palm up but not touching, not yet. Then I looked over at Zans and Bee.

The telepath was already unzipping the armor from her left arm, and Zans had pulled a knife.

We had to feed the spell to get it off Knox. Then we had to contain it. Or turn it back on its caster.

Bee and Zans stepped forward. Ignoring Knox writhing on the floor, the telekinetic steadied the telepath's arm and sliced shallowly just below her elbow.

Bee directed the blood so that it dripped into the palm of my hand. The magic contained within it tingled against my skin. The telepath stopped bleeding, withdrawing her arm.

"Is that enough?" she asked.

I met Fish's gaze. The sacrifice required was so extreme—a life for a life—that we'd only ever attempted to break a curse of this caliber once before. We had failed then. But Knox and Bee were tied together, and the curse was already confused. So we might have a better chance this time.

Fish nodded.

I imbued my magic into Bee's blood, just as I would have if it were still running in her veins. I amplified it, giving it depth and volume.

Then I rotated my hand, slamming my blood-and-magic-filled palm down on top of Fish's hand.

The combined magic—Fish's, Bee's, and mine—lashed around our hands. I pumped more and more energy into the casting. Fish reached down and ripped the curse from Knox's chest. With our hands still connected, Fish and I stood in tandem.

The curse curled around our hands, consuming the magic tied to Bee's blood.

"It's strong," I muttered.

"I need a blood circle, Bee," Fish said instead of answering. "Around my feet."

"But … but…" Bee stuttered.

"Just do it."

The telepath darted forward, slashing the knife across her arm again, just below the first wound. Walking around Fish, then ducking under our linked hands, she allowed her blood to drip, creating a ragged circle around Fish's feet.

The telepath stepped back.

"Let me have it," Fish said to me.

I didn't want to let the curse go. The named spell had almost eaten through the magic in my palm. And Fish was tied to Bee in the same way Knox was, the same way we all were.

The curse, trapped in a circle with him, could kill the nullifier.

"Trust me, Socks," he whispered.

I nodded, letting go of the magic and stepping back.

A nullifying field snapped into place between me and Fish. He crouched, gripping the curse, then lowered it until it touched the blood Bee had splattered on the floor. The curse eagerly slipped from Fish's fingers, spreading across the blood, consuming the magic stored within it.

Fish pulled a black wax pencil from his pocket, quickly inscribing another circle around the blood circle. He stepped back over both, then imbued the wax with his nullifying magic. A secondary ward snapped into place around the curse.

Fish took another step back, then another. We all waited, ready to defend ourselves if the curse wasn't satisfied with the amount of magic in Bee's blood.

"Black witch?" I asked.

Fish grunted. "Felt like it. Powerful."

"The overseer? Silver Pine?"

He shook his head. "Don't know. I've never gotten near enough to get a bead on her magic."

"It would make sense," Zans said. "Losing the Five on her watch isn't going to be easy to explain to the Collective."

Fish grimaced. "If I had more time and Socks's help, I might be able to nullify it."

"We don't have time," Zans said, wrapping a rune-marked bandage around Bee's arm. "Not if they're willing to throw named blood curses."

"She'll run out of sacrifices before she gets us all," Knox muttered, rubbing his chest. He was sitting, propped up on one arm. But he didn't look like he'd be walking any time soon.

"She?" I asked. "Did you get a glimpse of her then?"

He shook his head. "No. Just the death headed ... our way."

"I'd like to know whether or not it was the same magic as on the roof in LA. Is the black witch who threw this curse the summoner?"

Fish snorted with amusement. "You think you've got yourself a bona fide nemesis, Socks?"

I ignored him. "Let's move." I stopped myself from reaching for Knox. I needed my hands free, and he didn't need the magical boost. Cla5 had to be functional, not overwhelmed by his visions.

Zans got Knox over her shoulder and onto his feet. I stepped away to assess the stairwell for traps, though I knew that if Calhoun and Jackson had already passed through, they'd likely disabled anything that had been left behind.

"I wouldn't want it to be me," Zans muttered quietly. "Just me, standing between Socks and anything she wanted."

"Feeling sorry for the witch trying to kill us, Tek5?" Fish asked. "How softhearted of you."

"I don't give a shit about the witch. Fixating on Socks proves she's an idiot. I want the big guns."

Knox moaned lightly, pained. I glanced back, leveling a look at Zans for jostling him. She snapped her mouth shut on whatever else she was going to add to her rant of vengeance against the Collective.

We didn't have time to plan for our future just yet. We had to survive our present first.

EIGHT

THE STAIRWELL TO THE MAIN LEVEL HAD BEEN replaced with a swamp—complete with blackened, misshapen trees, stunted bushes I couldn't identify, and a stagnant smell of burned grease that made my stomach churn. Paisley, the demon puppy, coughed three times, then burrowed into the backpack, quivering.

"Pulled through from another dimension?" Bee asked in a whisper.

I nodded, but didn't linger to see what creatures might have been swimming within the swamp to confirm. Either way, it was another massive display of power from our adversary.

We wouldn't be able to climb to the main floor, as we'd planned. We'd have to go the long way.

Fish sealed the doorway behind us as we turned into the main corridor of level one. That first level of the compound below ground mostly housed various training facilities dedicated to specific disciplines, both magical and mundane.

The corridor appeared empty.

"Tactical unit. A dozen or more," Knox said, pushing himself off Zans's shoulder to stand. He swayed but didn't fall. "Middle of the hall."

I reached for the nearest door, opening and standing behind it. It was constructed out of reinforced steel coated in layers of magical fortification, so that spells could be practiced within safely. Well, safely for anyone in the corridor. Bee slipped in beside me.

Fish, Zans, and Knox did the same on the other side of the hall, slightly forward from my position.

I stepped partially into the room to my left so that I could eye the corridor before us through the thin opening between the door and the jamb. "Still looks clear," I whispered. "Bee?"

The telepath shook her head with a grimace. "Feedback."

They were blocking Bee, which was to be expected. And they were either mostly blocking Knox, or the death curse had consumed a lot of his magic.

But they were going to have a hard time blocking me. I'd yet to encounter a magical being who could stop me. Unfortunately, I had to lay hands on my victims.

I glanced over at Fish and Zans, speaking as quietly as I could while still being clear. "Frontal attack. Nul5 and I strip their shields, then—"

Knox gasped. His eyes flared white. "Now!"

I stepped to the center of the hall, reaching for Fish's outstretched hand. Nul5's magic lashed out, surrounding us. I pumped my magic into him, increasing his output. A shield snapped into place before us. Zans crossed to my other side, taking my free hand. I amplified her at the same time I did Fish.

The shield before us sparked at multiple points.

Gunfire.

Headshots, if they'd gotten through.

It was worth a try, but ultimately stupid.

The hall before us still appeared to be empty. The camouflage spell they were holding in place, along with what I assumed were multiple barrier spells, hadn't even rippled with the primary assault.

"Take out the shooters," I said.

Fish thrust his hand forward. His amplified nullifying power boiled down the corridor, shredding through the shielding the tactical team had thought would hold against us.

I caught sight of a half-dozen of the assault team as they scrambled, falling back, dragging screaming team members with them. I picked up magic from a mixture of sorcerers, shapeshifters, and at least one witch, but no one I immediately recognized. Whoever was holding the wards—likely multiple people, if they were planning to stand against the Five—got the camouflage and barrier spells back in place.

The lack of return gunfire indicated that the shooters had been incapacitated, likely from the backfiring of their own weapons. Weapons whose warding they had gambled on being strong enough to stand against the five of us united.

The spells blocking the assault team from my sight flickered. Imperfect now. Fish's assault had hurt the casters as well.

"Move," I murmured.

Zans, Fish, and I stepped forward as one, steadily closing the space between us and the shielded tactical team.

Bee and Knox slipped in behind us.

"They called for backup, another dozen," Knox muttered. "Too many. They'll be tripping over each other." He pressed his palm against my back, his power shifting across all four of my blood tattoos.

He sighed heavily. Then he started loosening the straps of the backpack holding the demon pup, Paisley.

I didn't question the clairvoyant. But I couldn't release Zans's or Fish's hands to help him.

A magical barrage hit us next. Spell after spell exploded against Fish's nullifying field.

Knox got the puppy loose. "Help me, Bee," he whispered.

I felt more than saw Bee get the backpack strapped frontways onto Knox. A chill twisted through me—both from the prolonged contact with the demon pup, and from the idea that Knox had seen the need for me to be unfettered.

Something massive struck the nullifying shield, exploding in a burst of magically fueled fire.

Fish stumbled. "Fuck!" His shield compressed around us for a moment. "They've been keeping that in their back pockets."

"Let me loose, Socks," Zans muttered. "Let me loose."

"Knox?" I asked.

"Not yet. I'm not seeing too clearly, but … it … it comes down to you, Socks. I think. Either that, or we're all about to die."

I glanced back at him.

He shrugged. "Like I said, there's a lot of magic being thrown, and it's not terribly clear what…" His eyes flared white suddenly. "Fish!"

Something hit the barrier right in front of the nullifier's face, resolving into a black splotch. Then it started drilling through the shield.

"Fish?" I asked.

He shook his head, his gaze pinned to the spell trying to make its way through the nullifying barrier toward him. Then he grimaced, starting to shake with the effort of keeping the spell at bay.

I tore my hand free from his grip, slamming my palm across his back instead. I pumped power into him directly through the blood tattoo that bound my magic to him.

The spell wormed its way through the shield, hitting Fish in the forehead. I pumped more magic into him as he reached up and wrapped his fingers, along with his magic, around the spell that was trying to attach itself to him.

Fish's shield contracted tightly around us. He couldn't spread it across the hall and fight the spell trying to kill him at the same time.

"That..." Zans murmured. "That shouldn't be possible. Not while he's amplified. Hit him over the head, poison him, or suffocation ... but..."

"They have our blood," I said grimly. "We're sitting ducks."

Another spell hit Fish's shield.

Knox grabbed for Bee, pulling her behind Fish, who was still fighting with the spell. The clairvoyant met my gaze.

I saw my death in his eyes. All of our deaths.

I pulled my blades, spinning to face the corridor. The tactical team's shield was battered, shredded in places. "Try to not bring down the corridor, Zans."

Tek5 nodded, flexing her hands.

"Fish?" I asked.

He grunted, indicating that he'd heard—and that he understood.

A second spell made it through Fish's nullifying field, slamming into Knox. Nul5 reached back with his other hand, trying to wrench it free of the clairvoyant.

"Give me a little push, Zans," I said. I crouched low, raising my blades before me.

She laughed, placing her hand on my back.

"Now!" I shouted.

Fish released his nullifying shield with a shove. It flooded through the hall, shredding the last of the defenses between us and our opponents—hopefully along with any magic they'd activated.

I sprang forward, leaping into the air. Zans's magic followed me, pushing me farther and faster than I could have leaped on my own.

I flew along the corridor, seeing the looks of horror dawning across the faces of the tactical team.

I tucked my knees to my chest, hitting the ground, then allowed the momentum to roll me forward, deep into the team scrambling to confront me.

Knox was right. They were tripping over themselves in the tight space.

I took the first two out with fast slashes to the midsection before I even gained my feet. Zans teleported in beside me. Her short range was deadly accurate if she could home in on one of the Five.

Our adversaries stumbled back. I took two more out, their magic dying on their lips, unarticulated.

Magic slammed against me, promising my death. Pain shrieked through my every nerve. I lost hold of my right blade, though it should have been magically tied to me. I managed to kill the caster responsible with my left.

Then I grabbed the face of the sorcerer closest to me, taking his magic. Every last drop. I fed his death to the spell attempting to claim me. He fell at my feet, a withered husk. Thankfully, whoever had cast the original spell hadn't tied the curse to me with blood and sacrifice.

The remaining members of the tactical team stumbled back in terror. Zans brushed her shoulder against mine. A sorcerer and a shapeshifter to my left started clawing at their throats, their collars appearing to choke them.

Bee screamed, still behind us.

I spun, leaving Zans to finish off the stragglers.

Bee was standing in the middle of the corridor. The telepath was shaking, her hands thrust before her. Fish and Knox were down behind her. But I could see the shimmer of a nullifying field, so Fish was still conscious.

Three of the tactical team had made it past Zans and me, or had teleported into the hall behind us. Bee was trying to hold them off.

I scooped up my fallen blade, already running.

Bee met my gaze. Then slowly, straining against whatever magic was attempting to hold her in place, she pointed to the witch on her left.

That witch spun around, meeting my gaze. She attempted to throw another spell at me.

She was either too slow or too drained, or was unable to maintain whatever she was doing to block Bee and cast at the same time.

Still running, I threw my blade—a sloppy move, though the weapon was well balanced. It managed to take the witch between the eyes. She fell.

Released from whatever power the witch had been holding against her, Bee's magic lashed out. She screamed. Her own power flooded the hall, battering against me.

Every single member of the tactical team who was still alive enough to feel Bee's wrath stiffened, convulsed, and fell to the floor, mouths foaming. Bee's telepathy had scrambled their minds.

Then they stilled. Brain-dead. Though their hearts would most likely beat for a little while longer.

Bee dropped to the ground, upright but spent.

Fish's shield compressed around him and Knox—then contracted specifically around the spells he was holding at bay in his hands.

I dashed toward him, wrenching my second blade out of the witch's head. Then I grabbed the two nearest sorcerers that Bee had felled, dragging them with me. Without thinking about what I was doing, I slashed and ripped the armor from the sorcerers' chests, offering my blade to Fish.

He nodded. Barely able to hold his head upright, he pressed his hands together, shaking and grunting until he managed to hold the two death curses in one hand. Then he took my blade and carved a pentagram in the chest of the sorcerer nearest to him.

"Knox first," I said.

The clairvoyant crawled to us, pushing up the sleeve of his sweatshirt. I held his arm over the pentagram carved into the skin of the sorcerer and bled him.

Fish traced the pentagram over and over, muttering and mixing the blood together. Then he fed Knox's death curse to the sorcerer Bee had incapacitated.

I repeated the process with the second sorcerer, Fish's blood, and the death curse meant for him.

Zans came striding down the hall, brushing her hands together. "I finished off what was left of the tactical team on this level," she said matter-of-factly. "Then I scouted ahead. The stairs are clear."

I cast my gaze around the corridor, counting twenty-two bodies. But we had another level to clear just to make it out of the building. And only Zans and I were fully functional.

"The black witch," I said, pointing toward the witch whose head I'd split open. "That wasn't her."

Zans shook her head grimly. "Nope."

"They'll have curses ready for you and me," I said. "Possibly more for the others, in case we thwart the first volley."

"She's killing someone with each curse she releases," Fish said wearily. "She's going to run out of people to sacrifice."

"I doubt they were volunteering," Zans said darkly.

Bee half crawled, half dragged herself over to Knox and Fish, pulling bandages out of her pockets and slapping them over the slashes where I'd bled them.

The demon puppy stuck her head out of the backpack still strapped to Knox's chest, panting happily.

"Zans and I go ahead, clearing the way—"

"No," Fish said. "We stick together. You're going to need us, Socks." He looked over at Knox grimly. "Isn't she?"

"Yeah." Knox petted the puppy gently. "We stick together. That much I see. We stick together until there's nothing left to see."

Silence settled over us as the understanding of what Knox was saying sank in. He wasn't seeing a future for us. Not beyond the next few moments. That could have meant anything, of course. But one of those many possibilities was that we were all going to die.

And then what would it all have been for? For what reason had we even existed in the first place? Just to be the pawns of the Collective? There was so much blood on our hands ... on my hands, specifically. Hands that had been designed, then trained, to kill. And I wasn't going to get a chance to make a different choice for myself.

"I refuse," I snarled. "I refuse to die here. Where they bred us, where they forced us to kill, to become murderers. They stole our childhoods."

"We wouldn't exist without them," Fish said, always practical.

"I don't give a shit," I said. "I'll die on my own terms. Outside. With the breeze and the sun on my face. Not in their prison, not under their control."

They all looked at me, startled by my overly emotional outburst.

Then Knox laughed quietly. "All right."

NINE

FISH WAS SO DRAINED FROM FIGHTING WHAT amounted to three named death curses in a row that he couldn't shield us and walk at the same time. Not even amplified by me. And according to the clairvoyant, I had to watch my own reserves as well. So Knox and Bee worked together to keep themselves mostly upright, and Zans carried Fish telekinetically.

Problem was, prolonged telekinesis and living tissue didn't mix well, usually resulting in internal organ damage. And that was when Zans was trying to wield her magic precisely. But twenty-one years of practice and the blood tattoos we all bore made carrying us aloft for short stints, or throwing me forward into a battle situation, easier.

Knox got enough glimpses of the immediate future to guide us through the literal minefield waiting for us on the final flight of stairs to the main level. Zans tossed anything the clairvoyant identified in our path—anything that couldn't just be avoided or neutralized by Fish—over the stairs and down into the depths of the compound. Magic raged at our backs as we finally climbed to the final level of the compound—the only part of the concrete-and-steel building that was above ground.

Then we were within viewing distance of the front entrance. The concrete gave way to windows and glass front doors. A large seating area with straight-backed couches and chairs. Even a few plants.

Unfortunately, the security checkpoint that sealed the entrance off from the outside world was occupied by what remained of the compound's tactical force, easily another two dozen people.

Plus one massively powerful black witch.

Our current overseer.

Silver Pine.

She stood about three strides this side of the magically fortified bulletproof glass that divided the front reception area from the main security check-point. She might have been anywhere from thirty-five to fifty. Age was difficult to estimate in those of the magical persuasion—and even more difficult with the amount of black energy seething from within and around her. She was standing barefoot in a dark cloud of power that writhed across the polished concrete floor in all directions.

She pinned her black-orbed eyes on me as I stepped up ahead of the other four. Deep-blue veins stood out from the pale skin of her neck, upper chest, arms, and lower legs. She was wearing a black silk crepe dress that was tattered from just above her knees to her ankles.

The dark cloud of power around her parted, giving me a momentary glimpse of the bodies arrayed around the black witch. They were wearing the compound's standard sweats. Cannon fodder. Without question, at least three had already been sacrificed to power the death curses Fish had thwarted. Maybe one more for the dimensional pocket that had blocked the stairwell to the main level, forcing us to take a path dictated by the overseer herself.

"I knew you were a problem from the moment of your birth, Amp5." Silver Pine's voice was laced with so much dark power that I had to suppress a shudder. "I begged the others to allow another amplifier to fully gestate. It would have made them the youngest of the fifth generation, but it would still have been manageable."

I took another step forward. Zans set Fish on his feet behind me, and he placed his hand on my back over my tattoos. His magic smoothed around me, shielding me tightly.

Silver's gaze flicked to the others, frowning as they stepped up tightly against me. The witch laughed harshly. "Do you honestly think the five of you are enough to get by one of the Collective?"

Within the darkness around her, I could suddenly make out creatures chittering, circling close. Demons at best guess, though I had never seen their specific type before. Sleek heads and spindly arms, possibly double-jointed. Sickle claws, powerful back legs. Somehow, as with the stairwell, the witch had summoned forth a pocket of another dimension, binding all the creatures within to her service.

Her malignant power expanded a few inches across the concrete floor. Then a few inches more. Muffled cries of pain seeped through to me.

The people on the floor...Silver's sacrifices...some of them were still alive.

I faltered a step.

Fish shifted his hand up to the base of my neck, practically cradling my head. Bee slipped her fingers in from my left, as Knox did the same from the right. They pressed against my back, over the individual blood tattoos that tied them to me.

Zans stepped in front of me. I touched her back, as the others were touching me. Allowing my magic to well up, but not pumping it into the telekinetic yet.

Fish's nullifying magic stretched out to cover all of us, chilling me through and through.

I welcomed the numbness.

I invited it.

Each of the three behind me were drained, their magic a whisper of what it usually was. I could power them up for a short burst. But I didn't think it would be enough to get us through the black witch as well as the team arrayed across the security checkpoint.

"Knox?" Fish asked in a whisper.

"It's up to Socks now," the clairvoyant said.

I swept my gaze across the security station, noting the face of every single person standing against me. Against us. They bristled with their individual power, ready to back the black witch.

She was, after all, the current overseer of the compound. The representative of the Collective.

Standing on the far right, Mark Calhoun and Becca Jackson were also behind the bulletproof glass. They were obviously under guard, but not bound. And only steps away from freedom. Their escape would be easily facilitated, given a big enough distraction.

I met each of their furious gazes. Then I smiled.

"What exactly is so funny when you're about to die, Amp5?" Silver Pine asked. "When you're about to take responsibility for the deaths of your entire generation?"

Fish chuckled. Then Knox and Bee joined him.

Zans glanced back at me.

Instead of addressing the black witch, who didn't deserve any more of my attention, I spoke to the tactical team standing behind her. "If you retreat now, I can't promise that you'll survive. But you will die if you remain."

"Oh, please—" the black witch started to snarl.

I slammed my magic into Zans.

The telekinetic flung her arms wide out to the sides. Her magic blasted out of her in a storm of steel as she let loose with the ball bearings she'd taken from the weapons cache, tearing through and shattering every piece of furniture between us and the witch. Then Zans brought her hands together, shattering the bulletproof glass from its outer edges in toward the center.

The tactical team beyond the glass rushed for cover.

Silver Pine stood within the black cloud of her power, untouched. Magic glinted from a curved steel knife as the black witch crouched to grab one of the humans arrayed around her feet, then slashed her throat.

I pumped more magic into Zans. She grunted, gathering the ball bearings, the shattered glass, and the broken pieces of furniture. Then she used that debris to pummel the shield the witch held around her.

An inky-scaled, ragged-toothed creature reached out of the dark magic seething around the witch. The demon ate her victim. But Silver Pine remained focused on whatever spell she was pooling in her hands. Another creature dragged another of the witch's sacrifices into the black pool of power.

I pushed Zans slightly. She stepped forward obligingly, continuing to batter all her magic against the black witch's formidable shielding. The four of us followed in tight formation.

I had to get to the witch, to lay hands on her, before she released the spell she was preparing.

Fish faltered. I paused so he could give me more of his weight.

"Zans," Knox whispered. "The spell is for Zans..."

I dropped my hold on Zans, spinning under and around Fish's arm so he stood between me and the telekinetic.

The black witch released the spell.

It sped toward us.

Fish wrapped his hands around Zans's shoulders, condensing his shield to concentrate solely around her.

I slammed my hand over the blood tattoo on his spine, amplifying him with everything I had. Bee shakily pulled her katana. Knox raised his shortsword. They crouched beside me, unshielded.

The spell hit Zans over her heart. She grunted, falling to her knees and dragging Fish with her.

Then I was the only one standing upright.

The ball bearings, the debris, and the glass shards that Zans had been holding all fell to the floor.

And for a moment, it was just me facing the black witch who had decided that I should die.

Why? I still had no idea.

And I didn't really care.

Because the front doors were open. The tactical team had fled. And through those doors, I could see daylight. And greenery.

Knox wrapped his hand around one of my bare calves, Bee around the other. Fish reached up to me, sliding his hand around the back of one knee.

I glanced down, meeting Zans's pained gaze. The black witch's named death curse writhed across her chest, trying to find a way through Fish's fading shield. A way to dig into her skin, to claim her life.

"You should know better, Silver Pine," I said, looking up to meet her self-satisfied gaze. "You've just handed me the way through your shield."

The witch scoffed. "You don't have that kind of power, Amp5. First, you'd have to be able to tear the blood curse from Tek5 before it kills her." She yanked another sacrifice victim before her curved steel blade. "And I'm already halfway to dropping you."

Zans convulsed. But snarling against the pain, she slid her hand up my leg, settling it next to Knox's.

I looked away. I looked past the destruction. I looked beyond the death the witch was preparing. My death.

It was sunny outside.

A breeze stirred the trees.

If I'd been closer, I might have been able to smell the air.

Was it moist and hot today? Dry and fragrant?

I let go. I released every barrier I held in place. Magic flared across my skin, down my limbs. Magic sparked between me and Bee, me and Knox, me and Zans, me and Fish, searing their skin to mine.

My arms floated to the sides as the magic rose through me, combining, intertwining. I gathered more and more power from the others, taking every last drop.

I closed my eyes, throwing my head back as I allowed the power to fill me, to have its way.

And for a moment, I was Bee. I could hear the thoughts of the others, including those of the people who'd fled from the building, trying to clear the compound or readying last defenses.

For a moment, I was Knox—seeing in flashes everything the witch was going to throw at me, seeing the hurricane I was about to create, seeing me wipe out everything in my path.

Then I was Zans—and all the debris rose again to whirl around us.

And finally, I was Fish—taking the nullifying power and wrapping it around us, protecting us from anything and everything.

Well, everything but me.

I was about to kill everyone.

And I was okay with that.

I opened my eyes, snapping my hands out to the sides. The gathered magic moved with me. I flicked my fingers, commanding the power into a whirlwind around us. Nothing touched us as the tornado I commanded ravaged the room.

Creatures—demons—boiled from the black magic pooled around the witch. Springing forward with claws and teeth, ready to rend me limb from limb.

Effortlessly, I caught them each, one at a time, with a lick of energy, pulling them into the tornado and tearing them apart. I would have stolen their magic as well, but it wasn't compatible. Or necessary.

My feet left the ground, until I was hovering a few inches above the floor. The others kept hold of me.

I reached out another lick of power, delicately. I caught the curse trying to kill Zans. I brought it even with me so I could whisper to it.

I met the gaze of the black witch, battering the edges of her shield with the whirlwind of power at my command.

I willed the tornado to move toward her, to carry us with it. It shifted forward, slipping around the witch's pool of black magic, chipping away at her defenses.

I paused a few steps away from her.

"Silver Pine," I said, my voice laden with magic not my own. "This death belongs to you."

I thrust my hand forward, slamming her with the death curse that had been named for Zans. The curse I had renamed, thereby turning it on its creator, against the barrier of magic she still held between us.

The curse slithered through her shield, striking her in the chest. She screamed, collapsing into the seething black cloud of magic she'd fed with blood sacrifices.

I didn't bother watching her die.

Thanks to Knox's clairvoyance, I knew that the compound's external defenses were about to be turned against us. And we'd have a better time surviving the onslaught outside of the concrete building.

I willed the tornado, the hurricane that was powered by all of us at once, to move. It tore through the entranceway, widening it as it transported us out of the building.

Magic pummeled my shielding, then explosions that were likely artillery. But the tornado of power consumed it all.

Knox's hand fell from my ankle. I paused, not wanting to lose him by moving any farther. Then Bee dropped away. And Zans.

I pumped more and more of myself into the magic swirling around us. We remained untouched.

Fish's hand fell away.

Unanchored, I drifted higher up into the vortex, fueling it. Losing control of the torrential power as it depleted the magic I'd gathered from the others … as it depleted me.

I threw my head back, adrift.

I could see blue sky above me.

I had made it out.

I would die on my own terms.

I'd be free.

The vortex tugged at me, draining the final licks of my power. I melted into it, giving it permission to consume me.

My first and last choice made solely for myself.

I was the vortex.

I was the Amplifier Protocol.

I slipped away, losing consciousness.

Death was peaceful and still.

And I wasn't alone within it.

TEN

THE GROUND WAS HARD. AND I WAS DESPERATELY hungry.

Something moist and smooth pressed against my right cheekbone. Then again.

I opened my eyes, blinking up at a deep-blue sky streaked by the last vestiges of a pink-and-orange sunrise. That was supposed to be some sort of warning, wasn't it? For sailors?

A blue-furred creature with a double row of sharply pointed teeth pounced on my chest. A long pinkish-blue tongue darted out of the little demon puppy's mouth, licking my nose.

That was decidedly unpleasant.

But for some unknown reason, laughter welled up in my chest. I scooped up the demon puppy—Paisley—and held her over my face. And I laughed.

Paisley twined her mane of tentacles around my fingers and chortled along with me.

Pressing the puppy against my chest, I sat up.

I was alive.

I could still feel the tender scars across my belly. My green dress was stained and torn in a dozen places, but I was otherwise unwounded. Knox, Bee, Zans, and Fish were sprawled unconscious around me. They were breathing, slowly but steadily, and didn't appear to be badly injured.

The immediate area around us had been flattened into a circle of hard-packed, scoured dirt about four meters in diameter. But beyond that...

Where there should have been concrete structures—the compound as well as some half-dozen outbuildings... where there should have been a twenty-foot-high, wire-topped perimeter fence... where there should have been vehicles and... and...

Nothing but devastation surrounded me.

I scrambled to my feet, clutching Paisley. Slowly pivoting, I could see nothing... nothing but the shredded remains of the facility and the foliage within which the compound had been hidden.

The puppy wiggled in my hands and I loosened my grip. She wiggled some more and I put her down. She hustled over to Knox, pressing her nose against his face, then darting back.

"No magic," I murmured as the realization hit me. I stretched my arms out before me. I felt... different. Weaker but healthy. Drained but not tired. I couldn't feel any magic from Knox or Bee or Zans or Fish.

I couldn't feel any magic from Paisley. The demon puppy currently looked like a regular gray-blue-furred dog. Yet I'd previously seen her tentacles, her red-hued eyes, and her too-wide, tooth-filled mouth. So she was some sort of shapeshifter, or she could mask her appearance. Either way, I should have been able to feel her magic, feel the magic that had drawn me to her in the depths of the compound.

I had drained myself. Completely. Utterly.

Had I also drained the others?

I had destroyed everything, all the way to the horizon. Buildings, trees, animals, people...

Knox sat up, rubbing his face and head with both hands. Paisley dashed around him, howling victoriously. He chuckled, then he paused, gazing down at his hands. He looked up at me. His expression was confused, incredulous.

"Socks?" he whispered. "You...you don't feel like you. And..." He trailed off, slowly standing as he cast his gaze around us, taking in the utter destruction I had wrought.

Fish woke up with a roar. One second, he was sprawled on the ground. The next, he was on his feet, fists raised, facing me.

I held my hands out, palms forward.

He faltered, shaking his head in confusion. "Socks?"

"Yes," Knox said.

Fish spun, reacting as if he was being attacked from behind. "What the hell is going on? How the fuck did you just…" His gaze fell on Zans to his right, still sprawled across the ground. Then he looked up to take in our surroundings. "…sneak up on…" He didn't finish the sentence.

Knox crouched down next to Bee, pressing his hand to her shoulder, then her cheek. She murmured under his touch, but didn't wake.

The clairvoyant looked up at me in wonderment. "Nothing. I feel … nothing."

I nodded, stepping over to retrieve one of my blades. I couldn't even remember hanging on to it. The second was still in my sheath.

Paisley wandered over and sat on my foot.

"You…" Fish looked at me. "You took it all? You have all our power?"

I shook my head, then I gestured around us. I still couldn't feel a drop of magic anywhere nearby. "I'm drained as well." Then a thought occurred to me, and I raised my hand to my neck. "Do … do I still have the tattoos?" I turned my back to Fish, carefully keeping my foot in place so as to not displace Paisley.

Fish stepped closer, brushing his fingers along the top of my spine. No magic stirred at his touch. I turned to face him, brushing his hand away with the move.

"They're still there," he murmured, locking his dark-eyed gaze to mine. "But they don't feel like anything." He reached up and brushed his fingers against the bare skin of my upper arm. "Just like skin. Your skin."

Zans rolled over onto her side, then sat up, muttering to herself disconcertedly.

Fish dropped his hand. "This isn't going to be good."

Zans raised her hands before her, clenching and unclenching them. Then she shrieked—an undulating, wild cry.

Bee woke with a gasp, grasping Knox's arm.

Zans pinned her gaze to me, rolling into a crouch, then raising her fists before her again. "You! You did this!" She screamed again, a terrible howl filled with pain and frustration. Her entire body shook with the emotion, the realization.

"That's enough," Bee shouted, scrambling on all fours to insert herself between Zans and me.

Zans took a shaking, gulping breath.

Bee pressed her hands to Zans's cheeks. She was smiling, practically glowing with joy. "We're free," she whispered. "We're finally free."

"We're nothing," Zans said. Her voice was a throaty growl, as if she'd damaged her vocal cords with her unnecessary shrieking. "We're nothing without our powers. She did this … she was always jealous—"

"No. That was you, Zans," Knox said mildly, stepping over to scoop up Paisley.

"We need to keep moving," I said. "Standing in the middle of a wasteland is a little exposed for my comfort."

Zans stood, dragging Bee with her. "You just destroyed everything around us. I think we're safe."

"We," Fish corrected. "We just destroyed everything."

"Fine," Zans snarled, eyeing me. "We. But that's the last choice you make for me, Amp5."

I laughed darkly. "No. It was the first choice you made for yourself, Tek5."

Zans's hands flexed as if she might have been contemplating hitting me.

I widened my smile. She had a couple of inches on me, but had always relied on her magic. Even drained, I was the stronger, better fighter.

"Fine," she repeated. "How do you suggest we find the fucking vehicle yard, assuming you haven't destroyed that as well—"

"We," Bee interjected. "We destroyed."

Zans inhaled deeply, then exhaled with a hiss. "There are no landmarks."

I pointed past her shoulder. "Except that."

She spun.

In the far, far distance, a red dot hovered just between the horizon and the rising sun. A balloon, at best guess. A flare would have left a streak in the air, and not lasted as long.

Zans looked over at Bee. "You had Jackson mark the location?"

Bee shook her head, then eyed me. "I'd guess Calhoun."

"So we didn't murder everyone," Knox said.

Using the red balloon as a guide, I started forward, picking my way carefully through the debris. If there were magical traps or adversaries lying in wait, I wouldn't feel them. But given the utter annihilation of our current surroundings, I was fairly certain the only thing threatening us was time. There was no way we could take down the compound and not draw attention from the remaining members of the Collective.

Still, I'd told Calhoun and Jackson that we'd meet them if possible. So there was a good chance that Bee was right. That Calhoun had left the beacon. In fact, I would have bet that what I saw as a red balloon was actually magical in nature. But I couldn't see or touch or feel magic anymore.

And I was okay with that.

AS WE STARTED THE LONG HIKE TOWARD THE RED balloon, I began to worry about how far the destruction of the vortex had gone. But as we walked on, the horizon slowly started to reveal the sight of wind-bent trees through the glare of the relentless sun.

When we finally drew close to those trees, Zans brushed past me, picking up the pace as the debris that had been hampering our progress eased away.

"What do you think?" Fish asked from behind me. "Five-kilometer radius?"

"Feels like it," Knox murmured. "So ten klicks ... with three of us drained, and Zans fighting a death curse."

Ten kilometers. And an indication that I would have been capable of wreaking far more destruction if those I'd drained had been at full capacity themselves.

"That would cripple a small city," Fish said. "Easily annihilate its downtown core." Keeping his pace steady, he reached down and scooped up a piece of twisted metal. "Well ... the Collective will be pleased."

He tossed the metal away, picking up his pace as well. He glanced at me sideways as he came abreast of me. "I imagine you're happier now that you agreed to help Zans destroy the place?"

"Sure," I said. "Give me the files you two got off the servers and I'll be blissful."

He laughed. "Nah, Socks. Blissful wouldn't suit you." He jogged away, following Zans beyond the tree line.

I paused, glancing up at the balloon just ahead of me now. It didn't appear to be tethered to the ground. "That's what magic looks like. When I can't see the energy that fuels it. A red balloon."

Bee laughed quietly, continuing through the trees after the other two.

Knox stepped up beside me. Paisley was perched on his shoulder, though she'd walked alongside me for most of the trek.

He touched my hand.

I pulled away automatically.

"It's a red balloon, Socks."

"Sure. Just floating by itself above the ground, unaffected by the wind."

He smiled grimly. "It'll come back. The magic. You've drained people before, fully."

"Killing them. Retaining the power for myself or funneling it into one of you."

"You figured how to take it without taking their lives."

I laughed. "Yeah. And how long do you think the Collective let them live after that? Who do you think the people the black witch sacrificed were? My victim pool. Bee's and mine."

"So maybe the magic doesn't come back. Does that idea relieve you? Do you think it would be easier to move forward without magic?"

"It would for you," I said, gazing at him thoughtfully. "Wouldn't it?"

"Most definitely."

"But you wouldn't be relieved."

He smiled softly. "No. But then, I believe in fate. Destiny. You and Fish don't. Bee and I do. Zans doesn't want to discuss it."

I laughed quietly.

He reached up and brushed his fingers against my cheek, then rubbed them together. "When was the last time I could touch you without glimpsing the future?"

I shook my head, not certain he'd ever been able to touch me that way. Not even after I learned to control and contain my magic.

A vehicle engine turned over, then caught somewhere nearby.

Knox passed Paisley to me, then held out his hand. "Come now. Let's go take a look at our future."

FOUR BLACK SUVS AND A GARAGE FILLED WITH SUP-plies stood in a fenced clearing between the trees. A single road ran out through an open gate. A few of the short-range electric ATVs used for patrolling the forest around the compound were neatly parked along the fence line. The red balloon hovered directly overhead.

The parking lot area was wide enough that it could have easily contained a dozen vehicles, and numerous relatively fresh tire tracks seemed to indicate that at least a few people had escaped. Hopefully that number included Becca and Mark, as the presence of the balloon suggested.

With the fate of the Five unknown, it was no surprise that they hadn't waited.

Zans pressed a bottle of water into my hands as she passed by, carrying supplies. She was loading the back of the nearest SUV.

I placed Paisley on the ground, crouching to pour water into my cupped palm for her to drink.

She eagerly lapped, splashing water all over my wrist and forearm.

Fish started another of the vehicles. He was systematically checking them, making certain they were operational and gassed up. Zans crossed back to the garage. Knox followed her.

Four vehicles.

Five of us.

We'd be strong, formidable, safer if we stuck together. But sticking together would only increase the size of the target on our backs. Even if our magic never returned.

I took a long swig of water, then gave Paisley another drink. She patted my palm with her paw, splashing the water playfully.

Knox wandered out, carrying two stuffed-full backpacks. He'd found a change of clothing. Blue jeans that were slightly too big for him, and a white T-shirt that made his skin appear more golden than usual. New tactical boots.

He tossed me a package of beef jerky as he carried the packs to the vehicle next to the SUV that Zans had been loading.

I ripped open the jerky, tearing off a piece and feeding it to Paisley. Then I took another long swig of water.

"Found it!" Bee cried from the depths of the garage. As she hustled out toward me, the sun glinted from her short-cropped yellow hair. She could grow it as long as she liked now.

And so could I.

I straightened as she approached. She had also changed, into a long cotton skirt and a green T-shirt. She was carrying a backpack over her shoulder, another pack in one hand, and a set of passports in her other hand.

The others stopped loading supplies into the vehicles, moving to join us. Zans was tugging a long bright-blue cotton dress over her armor. It fell past her knees.

Bee dropped the backpack at her feet, crouching to open it so we could see inside. It was full of bundled cash. American currency. Twenty-dollar bills.

Bee straightened, offering me one of the passports.

I took it, opening it to find a picture of a woman with shoulder-length red hair, pale skin, and bright green eyes.

No.

Not just any woman.

Me.

The Canadian passport had my Photoshopped picture in it.

That was what I would look like with hair.

I laughed involuntarily, then I looked at the name. Emma Johnson. "Emma. My name is Emma."

"Yeah," Bee said, passing out passports to Knox, Fish, and Zans. "Jackson and I were short on time, so we just ran down the popular names the year we were born."

"To blend in," I said, feeling oddly lightheaded.

"Christopher," Knox said.

Fish laughed. "Daniel."

We looked at Zans. She grimaced. "Samantha." She laughed, a little breathlessly.

"Amanda," Bee declared proudly. "Amanda Smith." She nudged the backpack with her foot. "And twenty thousand each to get us started. We didn't have time to get bank accounts or anything else set up. But the passports will get us across the border. Actually, being Canadian, we can travel just about anywhere in the world, even without visas."

I ran my thumb across the picture in the passport.

Emma.

Emma Johnson.

The other four were staring at me, patiently waiting. Waiting for me to deliver their final orders. I laughed, then I cleared my throat and stepped up. One last time.

"We each take an SUV. At the first opportunity, Fish heads north, Bee south, Zans east. I'll go west."

"And me?" Knox asked.

"You pick … Christopher. If your magic comes back, you need to be with one of us." I glanced at the others. They nodded in agreement.

He nodded, looking down at the passport in his hands. "I'll go with you, Emma."

Some sort of heat bloomed in my chest. A sort of pleasure. At being named.

"And that's it?" Fish asked flatly. "That's all?"

"Together, we're bigger targets," Zans said.

"And if we need each other?" Bee asked.

"Don't," I said. "Don't need us."

She looked at me steadily. "So when we do need you? You won't come?"

I wanted to say no. I wanted to walk away and never look back.

But if one of them called, I knew I would go. It was in my breeding, after all.

"I'll come."

"How are we supposed to find each other?" Fish said, his tone becoming heated. His gaze was on me.

"Paisley," Zans said. "Paisley was bred to be able to find us. So? Who gets the dog?"

"She goes with whoever she chooses," I said.

Zans nodded, crouching to pluck her share of the bundled cash out of Bee's bag. Then she crossed over to the nearest SUV and shut the back hatch. She turned back, looked at us, then down at the demon puppy at my feet.

"Hey, Paisley," she said in the most pleasant tone I'd ever heard from her. "You want to come with me?" She patted her thigh.

Paisley wiggled her butt, gamboling around in a circle. But then she just flopped down and panted.

Zans laughed snarkily. Then she glanced at all of us in turn, resting her gaze on me. "Today is gone," she said. "Today was fun."

"Tomorrow is another one," I said, finishing the quote from the children's book from which Knox had nicknamed the telekinetic.

She laughed, climbing into the SUV.

Bee fished her share of the cash out of the bag, tucking it into the backpack she'd been carrying. She pressed a kiss to my cheek, then to Fish's. She lingered to kiss Knox deeply. I glanced away.

"Paisley?" Bee asked, crouching down to scratch the demon puppy on the top of her head. Paisley accepted the caress, but didn't follow Bee as she straightened and stepped away without another word.

Zans backed out of her parking spot, lifting her hand in a wave as Bee darted around to the third-farthest SUV, shut the hatch, and climbed in.

Before I'd even seen him move, Fish pulled me forward into a crushing kiss. I accepted the gesture, feeling the anger behind the embrace even without my empathy powers.

I pressed my hand against his chest. He didn't loosen his hold. I gave him a more forceful push. He grunted, frustrated. But he stepped back, keeping hold of my upper arms. Too tightly.

He swept my face with a dark eyed gaze. "That's it, then?"

I didn't answer. The question was rhetorical. The decision already made.

He laughed. "I give you six months, Amp5. By then—"

"Emma," I said coolly. "My name is Emma."

He looked shocked, as if I'd slapped him.

He stepped back, dropping his hands. Then he shook his head. "Why should I be surprised? It was always on your terms, wasn't it?"

"No, Daniel. We all made the best of the situation. I didn't come to you expecting anything other than that moment. Just like I didn't question when you chose to have similar moments of intimacy with Bee, Zans, and Knox." I glanced over at Knox. He was watching Fish steadily.

I looked back at Fish.

He smiled wryly. "Some jealousy would have been appreciated."

"I'm not certain I have the capacity for it."

Knox stepped forward, hugging Fish. They thumped each other on the backs, murmuring quietly.

Bee backed her SUV out of its spot, following Zans out through the gate.

Knox broke the embrace, scooping up the backpack with the cash, then fishing out a few bundles and handing them to Fish. Then he zipped up the pack, slinging it over his shoulder. He wandered over to the SUV he'd already loaded with two other backpacks.

Two.

Knox had already known he was coming with one of us. And I had been the only one not putting together a pack for myself. So even without magic, he'd glimpsed our future.

"Come on, Paisley," Knox called over his shoulder. "Give Socks a minute."

The demon puppy licked my ankle. Then she hustled after Knox. He picked her up and climbed into the passenger side of the SUV.

I glanced back at Fish.

He grinned. "Six months. You've got the means to find me, with or without magic. I'll be waiting."

I laughed. "Don't wait, Fish."

He snorted, turning on his heel and climbing into the final SUV. He drove out through the gate as I crossed to join Knox.

Climbing into the plush seats of the SUV, I glanced over at Knox and Paisley. Both were chewing on beef jerky.

"So…" Knox said. "West?"

ZANS AND BEE WERE WAITING FOR US A LITTLE WAYS down the road, taking off again as the last two SUVs pulled up to follow them. At the first crossroads, Zans turned right, heading east. Bee turned left, heading west to find the next main road running south. I followed Fish for another few klicks until we reached the next chance to turn off.

Up ahead of us, Fish slowed to a stop. I couldn't see him through the tinted windows of his SUV, but he waited long enough that I could have opened my door and called out to him.

I didn't.

He continued on, heading north.

I turned left.

West.

The road stretched out before us. Christopher reached forward, fiddling with the stereo until he found some music. I didn't recognize the tune, but I had nothing to compare it to. Pop or rock of some sort.

"Where to?" he asked, leaning his head back and watching the empty road before us with a slight smile.

"The coast," I said, making the decision in the moment. "Then north. Across the border."

"Then bank accounts and credit cards."

"Sure. But first I want to walk on a beach … and eat ice cream. In a cone."

Christopher laughed quietly. "And then? The world is ours?"

"For as long and as far as we get."

"And you don't mind dragging me with you?"

I glanced over at him. He gazed back at me seriously. Then Paisley started chewing on his finger and he laughed.

"I'm … I'm glad I'm not alone," I said. To my own surprise, I meant it. "And I'm glad it was you and Paisley who chose me."

He laughed quietly. "They would have all chosen you, Fox in Socks. Even Zans. Without you…" He looked away out the side window, not finishing the thought.

I didn't push him to elaborate.

I gazed down the road before us, pressing my foot to the gas just a little bit harder. Eager for the next moment, the next experience, the next choice.

And if the magic didn't come back?

I wouldn't mind. Not one bit.

Close to Home

THE AMPLIFIER SERIES: BOOK 0.5

Sunflower

FREEDOM

Author's Note

Close to Home is a prequel novelette for the Amplifier series, which is set in the same universe as the Dowser, Oracle, and Reconstructionist series.

Gravel crunched out front, pulling my attention from the grimoire I was still trying to figure out how to read, let alone understand. It was one of three books my lawyer had sourced for me without questioning the content—magical transference. Or at least that was what was supposedly written within the leather-bound, handwritten tome. I was still working out a key and waiting for a couple of additional sorcery texts that I hoped would be able to help me piece together the rune-based language.

Sorcerers liked their secrets.

Not that I could cast any of the spells or incantations the grimoire supposedly held. Though I might have possessed an excess of power, knowledge was an armor I was severely lacking.

I untucked my legs from the afghan and rose from the couch, glancing out the side windows as I crossed through the front sitting room. The fire had burned down to bright-orange embers in the white-painted brick fireplace, but the refurbished fir flooring was still toasty warm under my bare feet.

Out the window, I spotted Christopher in the middle of the garden. He'd been methodically digging in compost for the past few days, in between long stints of hovering over the three-week-old chicks in the barn. It was overcast but not raining. Yet. With his earbuds in, he would have missed the sound of the car pulling up. But if the visitor heralded some kind of magical assault, the clairvoyant would have picked it up before the car had even turned into the driveway.

I glanced out the front window.

An RCMP SUV cruiser rolled to a stop, parking before the front walk to the house. A dark-haired uniformed officer stepped out, her attention on the barn. I followed her gaze to the back end of my 1967 light-blue Mustang convertible. Christopher had left the double-wide barn doors open.

The officer smirked, telling me everything I didn't already know about her with a single disdainful expression.

I crossed out of the front room and into the foyer, opening the front door and letting in a chilly breeze before she could step away from the cruiser.

She flinched, spinning on me and baring her teeth.

Shapeshifter.

She was in her midthirties. Dark brown hair pulled back in a messy bun. About five foot nine inches tall, slim and muscular, with naturally lightly tanned skin.

I'd expected a visit the previous November. The fact that it had taken the shifter—an officer of mundane law—over three months to drop by the home of new residents with as much magic as Christopher and

I carried further informed my opinion of her. Even more so than her sneering at my vehicle, and the suggestion that she thought a convertible was a frivolous choice of vehicle given the amount of rainfall Lake Cowichan, British Columbia, Canada experienced.

It had taken us almost seven years, but Christopher and I had gone west—and were now about as far west as we could get without leaving the continent.

I leaned against the doorframe, mostly closing the door behind me so I didn't let out all the warm air. As well as letting the shifter know that she wasn't going to be entering my home.

"Officer." I gave her a neutral smile, as was apparently expected of me in a small-town environment. Though the random drop-ins from the locals had lulled after the first two weeks of us moving in, even that had given me far too much practice at being pleasant but distant enough to not invite additional visits. Also, once our neighbors had gotten a good look at Paisley, they hadn't been quite so eager to cross through the gate that I kept purposely closed at the top of the drive.

The RCMP officer skirted the cruiser, making her way to the front walk, then jogging up onto the front patio.

She didn't offer her hand.

As expected.

Those of the magical persuasion rarely touched. And anyone with any magical sense didn't volunteer to touch me. In the years since I'd been free of the Collective, any contact with me was usually requested—then granted via a legally and magically binding contract. If I was satisfied with the terms and remuneration.

I was rarely satisfied. And I was not at all interested in taking on any more contracts. As a result, I rarely touched anyone with any magic thrumming through their veins.

The shifter swept a light-brown-eyed gaze over me, coming up unimpressed. "Emma Johnson?"

"I am she."

She cocked her head to the side. "Little cold for a sundress, isn't it?"

"Not until you disturbed my perfectly pleasant afternoon." I made a show of glancing at her name tag, though I'd already known everything I needed to know about her even before I bought the property. "Officer Raymond." She wasn't affiliated with any pack. And even more unusual was that she appeared to only run in the woods that bordered Lake Cowichan on all sides when she was forced to do so by the full moon. Most shapeshifters could transform at will no matter what the phase of the moon.

Tension ran through her jaw at my tone, but she couldn't hold my gaze for more than a few seconds.

Not a werewolf, then.

I hadn't been rude enough to actually spy on her while she was transforming—other than to make note of her routine and the tenor of her magic. And I'd been just as systematic with all the other main residents of the small town since we'd moved in three months before. Officer Raymond was the only Adept in Lake Cowichan proper. But even though she plainly wasn't a werewolf—her inability to hold my gaze made that obvious—it was still my guess that she transformed into some sort of canine.

"Hannah Stewart is … missing," she said.

The abrupt segue momentarily threw me.

Hannah Stewart. Early twenties. Medium-length light-brown hair, medium-blue eyes, glasses. About five foot six. She ran the thrift store. I'd seen her two days before when I'd picked up the cashmere cardigan I'd left on the back of the couch in the sitting room. The fire had warmed the room too much to continue wearing it.

I frowned. "And you expected to find her here?"

"No … I … " The shifter cleared her throat, glancing away toward the garden that spread out from the east side of the main house.

I kept my gaze on her, watching her struggle with whatever concern or request had brought her to the doorstep of an unknown Adept.

She nodded to herself, then met my gaze resolutely.

"I know you … both of you … are some kind of witches."

I didn't answer.

She didn't elaborate.

Silence stretched between us long enough that I started to feel chilly. Officer Raymond glanced away, looking toward the garden again, then shifting her booted feet on the patio and glancing to the other side, toward the Wilsons' property. A stand of cedar bushes cultivated into unnatural shapes by the resident deer blocked the view of the neighbors' house, but I could see their milk cows in the front adjacent field. They rotated the livestock every few weeks, though I was fairly certain that mid-February was still too early for the grass to grow.

"I know it's rude," the shifter said, speaking as if we hadn't just been standing in chilly silence for far too long. Her tone hardened, becoming edged with some emotion I couldn't place. "I know Adepts have rules. And that you're obviously... not out. Maybe not practicing? Wanting to stay off the coven's radar? I know there's a coven in Vancouver. And another witch on Salt Spring Island."

She glanced at me.

I didn't react.

"I saw Tyler Grant hightailing it out of town last night in his junker. Hannah didn't open the thrift shop this morning. I've tried her apartment and knocked on the Grants' door about an hour ago ..." She trailed off. "I'd like you to ... cast a finding for her."

Her hesitation before mentioning magic made it clear she was woefully ignorant. Not because she didn't know the proper terminology, but because no one had taught her that there wasn't any uniform system of magic.

And I wasn't the mentoring type.

"What's wrong with your nose, shifter?" I asked mildly.

She stiffened, then glared at my left shoulder instead of meeting my gaze.

I shook my head, pushing the door open behind me just enough to step back into the house. "We aren't witches. Which I suppose answers my own question about your scenting abilities. We'll keep to ourselves, and you'll do the same."

"And if I don't?"

I swung the door shut, slowing it so it clicked closed gently between us rather than slamming. Officer Raymond—who still hadn't properly identified herself—stared at me through the inset glass panel, clenching and unclenching her hands.

Then her gaze shifted just over my shoulder.

Christopher had slipped into the hall behind me. I could feel the steady hum of his magic, but nothing that indicated he was in the middle of a vision, so I kept my gaze on the shifter on the patio.

The clairvoyant stepped up behind me. Officer Raymond's gaze softened as she took him in—white-blond hair, gray eyes, golden skin, standing just shy of six feet tall. It was a subtle change in the shifter's expression, but I caught it.

It was difficult to look at Christopher for more than a moment before realizing he was beautiful. Though I hadn't been made aware of that myself until we'd spent some time in the real world—outside the imposed confines of the compound that had been our only home for more than twenty years. 'Otherworldly,' I'd heard people whisper after laying eyes on him.

But to me, the clairvoyant was and always would be my brother, though as far as we knew, we shared no DNA. The identical last names on our passports—chosen by Bee as if the telepath had known that we'd remain together after leaving the compound—could have indicated a sexual partnership. But even through the time that our magic had been drained enough to allow for the possibility of intimacy, that was a line we had never blurred.

Still, I understood why people stared or stuttered around Christopher. Even those who couldn't pick up the tenor of his magic. And though our coloring was vastly different, I occasionally garnered the same reaction. Until I met the gaze of my admirer. Then the whispers or admiration abruptly stopped.

"Hannah Stewart is missing," Christopher said.

I glanced at him. He'd never met Hannah. He hadn't left the property since we'd moved in, which had been the primary point of purchasing a house situated on just over two hectares in a remote location in the first place. Five acres, the neighbors still called it, with their seemingly arbitrary tendency to switch between metric and imperial measurements.

"You saw or you overheard?" I asked.

"Overheard."

"Hannah's boyfriend left town." I settled back into my staring contest with the shifter on the front patio. "Officer Raymond is jumping to conclusions."

"Officer Raymond has magically honed instincts."

I snorted. "She's not that kind of shapeshifter."

"Because she thought we were witches?"

I didn't answer.

"Come on, Socks. That's a narrow view. What are the chances she's ever scented a … Adepts like us?"

He had hesitated before naming our main classifications—amplifier and clairvoyant. Even if her nose sucked, chances were that Officer Raymond could hear our conversation through the single-paned glass door.

"You mean us to stay," he said. "You want us to stay, yes?"

I did. He already knew that.

Christopher padded forward, moving like a highly skilled martial artist who'd cloaked himself in dirty jeans and an old T-shirt. He'd rolled up the legs of the jeans, exposing his ankles. His feet were bare but scrubbed clean. He refused to wear the gumboots I'd ordered for him for gardening.

The clairvoyant opened the door, allowing another cold gust of wind into the foyer. "Officer," he said. Then he glanced back at me.

I was about to be completely undermined. I turned away, crossing into the front sitting room to retrieve my cardigan.

"I'm Christopher Johnson, Emma's brother."

"Oh … " The shifter's attitude melted under the onslaught of everything that Christopher leaked. Beauty, charisma, magic. Or maybe she was just reacting to the indication that he and I were siblings, not lovers. "I'm ... Jenni ... " She paused, gathering herself. "Constable Jennifer Raymond."

If she touched him, if he allowed her to touch him, he might be inundated with visions for days. Though it was apparent her magic wasn't particularly strong, so I could hope I was wrong about that.

And it was none of my business who Christopher chose to interact with. I wasn't his jailer. Just his ... custodian.

I pulled on my sweater, focusing on the soft brush of the worn cashmere over the skin of my arms and across the blood tattoos simmering with magic on my spine, hidden under my hair.

"Please come in," Christopher said in the foyer. "Emma will put on tea."

I glanced at the wooden clock on the mantel in annoyance—a relic of the former owners that I'd ex-cavated from the attic. It was two hours away from afternoon tea. We'd eaten lunch only an hour before.

"I ... I just need to grab something from the car," Officer Raymond said. She was still a little breathless, especially for a supposedly well-trained RCMP of-ficer who was about to enter the house of powerful Adepts.

Of course, she thought we were nonpracticing witches without a coven.

The front door clicked shut. Then Christopher stepped back, leaning in the open archway between the foyer and the sitting room. He crossed his arms and settled his gaze on me.

I checked his eyes for signs of magic, seeing none.

"You know that you're going to have to meet more people, beyond the real estate agent and the grocery delivery guy. If we're staying."

I jutted out my chin. "I already said I'd start going to the diner for lunch once a week."

"But you haven't. And Hannah Stewart is on the very short list of people you know in town. You bought that sweater from her two days ago."

"Cardigan."

Christopher laughed softly.

Buttoning the top three buttons of the afore-mentioned article of clothing, I turned away, crossing back through the house into the kitchen. Christopher followed me.

Paisley was sprawled across the three-foot-by-four-foot gray-speckled white quartz counter of the kitchen island—and practically covering all its available space. The blue-gray demon dog was resting her chin on an overturned roasting pan. The roasting pan that had been in the fridge. The pan that had formerly held yesterday's leftover roast chicken. Catching my gaze with her dark-red eyes, Paisley snapped her double row of sharply pointed teeth playfully, then struck the roasting pan hard with a clawed paw the size of a small plate.

The pan spun toward me.

I caught it. It was licked clean.

Christopher laughed.

I gave the demon dog on the counter a look. "We have company."

Paisley, currently the size of a large mastiff and bearing a mane of tentacles, stretched as magic writhed across her blue-furred skin. She leaped off the counter, hitting the tiled floor front paws first while transforming into her blue-nosed pit bull aspect—without the red eyes and tentacles that marked her as a half-demon. She flashed her double row of teeth at me, then gently took the roasting pan in her mouth and carried it over to the sink.

The front door opened.

Ignoring the disconcerting feeling of shifter magic entering the house, I plucked the stainless steel kettle off the stove and crossed to the sink to fill it. Then I squirted dish soap into the roasting pan and let it fill with hot water.

Hands in the front pockets of his jeans, Christopher wandered past the kitchen table over to the double French doors, gazing out at the backyard and garden. Paisley joined him.

I set the kettle down on the stove, turning the gas burner to high then stepping back to turn off the water.

Officer Raymond stepped into the kitchen from the hall. Her gaze flicked around, obviously impressed.

I'd had the fir floors throughout the three-storey house sanded and varnished before we'd moved in, then had the entire house painted white—inside and out, including the attics. But as far as renovations went, the kitchen was the only room that had been gutted and modernized.

For Christopher.

I didn't cook. I occasionally liked to bake. But the thirty-year-old oven we'd pulled out would have been fine for that.

Likewise, replacing the old moss-covered roof with red metal had been a perfectly practical decision on my part, and had nothing to do with any silly notion about living in a picturesque farmhouse.

Most of the furniture in the house had been left by the previous owners after they'd died, but had been picked over enough by various relatives that a few of the rooms remained empty. That included three of the upstairs bedrooms, the dining room, and what I thought might have once been a study, given the built-in bookshelves. Accumulating belongings was a foreign and uncomfortable experience that I preferred to ignore, beyond the little we needed to be functional. It had taken three years to find a property where Christopher could roam freely without a constant influx of energy from random people.

Such as the shapeshifter currently invading my home.

Ignoring the RCMP officer as she crossed to the island and set a plastic-wrapped item on one of the stools, I retrieved a plate for cookies, three matching earthenware mugs, and the teapot. We only had a set of four of the mugs, purchased from a local potter.

I had baked an entire batch of ginger snaps by Christopher's request earlier that morning, instead of rolling and freezing the batter as I usually would have. I threw the back of the clairvoyant's head a peeved look. Apparently, he'd known we'd be having a visitor. A bit of a heads-up would have been ideal, though I never pushed Christopher to divulge if it wasn't necessary. Because the deliberate application of his magic often triggered an onslaught of clairvoyant power.

It had taken over a year after the complete annihilation of the compound for my magic to seep back. Christopher had gone almost a year and a half without a glimpse of the future. Unfortunately for the clairvoyant, his magic had come back punishingly powerful, even more so than before, making entire swaths of his life dysfunctional. He'd be fine for weeks, months even, able to hold down a kitchen job in a restaurant, go grocery shopping, take Paisley for walks. Then I'd come back to whatever city apartment we were renting to find him hiding in a closet, completely overwhelmed by the future echoes of the life of an Adept he'd inadvertently come into contact with.

And of course, my amplification magic was far from a calming influence.

The presence of the other three of the Five we had once been—and of Fish's nullifying power especially—might have helped balance Christopher. It might have spread the visions and glimpses of the future equally among us, tied through our blood tattoos. But even anchored by Bee's telepathy or Zans's telekinesis, I wasn't certain that controlling Christopher's power was even possible anymore, given how strong his magic had grown while it had been slumbering in his veins, playing possum.

A half-dozen incidents with Christopher had forced us to move multiple times, for fear of the Collective tracking us down through any network that might make note of possible clairvoyant activity. So I had made a decision to take on jobs under a false name. Over the course of five such assignments, I had cultivated a reputation I'd never wanted—a powerful amplifier who was willing to work for the highest bidder—so that I could purchase a new life for us. This sanctuary.

We'd had three months in Lake Cowichan. Three months without incident, without wondering if we needed to run. Three months was enough to begin to hope. And hope was dangerous for people of our power, of our upbringing. I knew. Because I knew what I was capable of doing with only a glimmer of hope to guide me.

Now Constable Jennifer Raymond was in my kitchen. About to drink my meticulously curated tea, my painstakingly tested ginger snaps—

The kettle whistled.

I stepped over without looking, removing the kettle from the heat and turning off the burner.

"I ... I don't mean to intrude," Officer Raymond said.

But her gaze was on Christopher, not me, so I measured three teaspoons of Tanzania Estate tea into the strainer and didn't respond.

It wasn't an apology. It was just one of those things that people said, things they didn't mean. I loathed that about human interaction.

I stepped back, put the stovetop timer on for three minutes—I preferred to not oversteep black tea—then set out the milk and sugar, along with three side plates and white napkins with a blue lace border.

I'd bought the napkins from Hannah. At the thrift store.

Damn it.

The shifter was more observant than I'd given her credit for. She must have seen me coming and going from the store, seen me chatting with Hannah. And now she wanted to capitalize on that observed behavior, that perceived relationship.

I arranged the tea and cookies on the corner of the kitchen island. The timer went off. I removed the strainer from the teapot.

Christopher turned from the window, crossing into the kitchen.

Officer Raymond watched him, enraptured.

I leaned back on the counter by the sink, arms folded as I tried to see what she saw. With the white-painted French-paned glass doors behind him and the overcast day beyond, he must have looked like ... pure light.

Paisley padded alongside Christopher.

"Oh, hello," Officer Raymond cooed, as if she'd just spotted the huge pit bull.

For her sake, I really hoped that wasn't the case. She had to just be playing another game, pretending to not have noticed the lethal predator prowling toward her. Because even beyond the deplorable lack of shifter instincts this revealed, it suggested she was completely unsuited to her choice of career, policing mundanes. Never mind what it said about her standing in the house of two powerful Adepts—and about to beg a favor from them.

The shifter waggled her fingers at Paisley, offering to pet her. The demon dog snorted derisively, then settled under the plate of cookies to gaze up at Christopher like he ruled her world. It was an effective technique, since not only was she hoping he wouldn't begrudge the unsanctioned consumption of the leftover roast chicken, but also she wanted ginger snaps.

Officer Raymond frowned at Paisley, brushing her hands on her pants and straightening. Her reaction time was human slow. She kept her beast firmly caged, which was negligent for many different reasons. If I actually had been a coven witch, I would have been placing a call into the closest West Coast pack representative immediately after meeting Officer Raymond. A shapeshifter who ignored their beast, and who didn't have the structure of a pack to guide them, was liable to snap. A loss of control could mean the loss of lives. And way too much attention drawn our way as a result.

"Milk?" Christopher asked Officer Raymond, going through the motions of serving the tea. He knew that I wouldn't do it, and that she wouldn't know that she was supposed to fix her own after he poured her cup.

She pursed her lips thoughtfully, then nodded.

He added a slosh of milk, handing the mug to her.

She reached for it, her left hand encircling the stoneware mug. Then her right hand moved beyond—to touch Christopher's forearm.

The gesture could have been completely harmless. She could have been flirting or simply saying thank you.

But I stepped forward nonetheless, reaching across the island over the teapot and cookies to snag her wrist.

Christopher steadied the mug he was still half holding.

The shifter reacted to my movement, then to me grabbing her. Completely delayed. She tried to yank her arm away but couldn't break my hold.

Her eyes widened, nostrils flaring. "You dare!"

"No," I said calmly. "You dare." I flicked my gaze to Christopher, then back to her.

"Let me go."

I almost forced her to try to break my hold. I almost goaded her into trying.

"Socks," Christopher whispered. The white of his magic flared, edging his eyes then fading.

I dropped Officer Raymond's wrist and was back leaning against the counter before she realized she was free.

She stared at me, then at Christopher, rubbing her wrist. Though if she was actually hurt, it was due to her feeble attempt to break my grasp, not the hold itself. "You aren't a witch," she said accusingly.

I didn't answer. That should have been obvious the moment she'd first scented me. In town. Over three months ago.

Christopher set her tea down next to her elbow. He poured a second mug, stirring in a teaspoon of sugar for me. And then a mug for himself, leaving it black. "Tell us about Hannah. And how you'd like us to help."

The shapeshifter stared at us, emotions ranging from surprise to confusion flitting over her face.

There really was no way she was a werewolf. Even if it was judgemental of me to look down on her for not using her magic.

"I'm not well versed in Adept society … " I said, reaching for my tea. "But even I know that you don't touch anyone without express permission."

"I would never."

I pinned the shifter with a withering gaze.

She looked away, sipping her tea. Then she grimaced.

Grimaced.

As if she hated the taste of my tea.

"Socks," Christopher murmured again.

I took a sip of my own tea. I was triggering his magic with my anger.

"I'm sorry," the shifter said. "We've gotten off on the wrong foot."

"Touching me comes with consequences," Christopher said, his tone steady and calm.

I hated that he felt he had to step in, to explain me, to explain himself. But that was always the way with us, between us. He was the fixer. I tore everything apart—but only after rationally assessing that it needed to be pulled asunder.

"And if you want us to find Hannah," he continued, "then those consequences could obscure my ability to help."

"She's a mundane," I said, grumbling into my tea. And completely lying. Hannah Stewart's blood held a faint trace of witch magic, likely inherited from way back. Similar to how any number of people in this part of Canada carried First Nations' blood. But dormant magic wasn't going to help Christopher key in on Hannah Stewart.

"I thought of that," the shifter said, picking up the item she'd retrieved from the cruiser. It was a ziplock bag that unrolled in her grasp, revealing a blue plastic comb within its depths.

"I see," I said, taking another sip of tea. "The ziplock makes it seem so official."

Officer Raymond clenched her jaw, as if she might be considering leaping across the island counter and slapping me.

I took another sip, letting her think about it.

She decided to remain on the edge of civil.

Too bad.

Paisley snatched the plastic-swathed comb from Officer Raymond and swallowed it whole, ziplock bag and all.

The shifter stumbled back. "What the fuck?!"

Paisley chortled darkly. Even after living with the demon dog for almost seven years, the sound sent a sliver of a chill down my spine.

Officer Raymond rubbed the back of her neck, staring at Paisley dumbfounded. Then she got angry. "That isn't a dog!"

"Just noticed that, did you?" I asked mockingly. Then I tapped my nose. "Now I see why you're a pack reject. Can't even find a woman in a small town when you have a sample of her hair."

The shifter turned bright red in fury.

I waited, just long enough to see if anything interesting was going to happen.

She sputtered, clenching and unclenching her fists. Then she got herself under control.

So, no.

Christopher took a sip of his tea, then spoke thoughtfully. "It has been raining."

Ever the peacemaker.

"For months," I said agreeably.

"Are you going to help or not?" The shifter spat out each word as if they were separate sentences.

"No," I said.

"Yes," Christopher said.

"The woman is a mundane." I set my mug down, crossing my arms.

"Hannah," Officer Raymond interjected, gazing hopefully at Christopher. "Her name is Hannah. And she has an abusive boyfriend."

"If you had any credible evidence that she was in trouble, you wouldn't be here with a comb in a ziplock bag."

"Yeah ... well, I might not have an official missing persons report. She's an adult, living on her own. Her mother in Victoria wasn't expecting her this weekend, and the few friends I could call haven't seen her. But since she took over running it, she's never not opened the store without leaving a note or it being a stat holiday. Even then ... " Officer Raymond clenched her fists. "I know ... I know something is wrong."

And for the first time, her shapeshifter magic coiled around her—a slight trickle of energy. Then it settled. So ... her magic was triggered by protective instinct, not in anger or in frustration.

I sighed inwardly. First Christopher's insistence, then Paisley with the comb, and now evidence that Officer Raymond wasn't a total magical dud.

Hannah Stewart was in trouble.

"We'll discuss it," I said.

The shifter glanced at her watch. "A small group of us are meeting at the diner at three for an unofficial search party. I can get you another DNA sample. If you cast a ... spell of finding, then meet with us but go your own way, it'll seem totally plausible when you find Hannah."

Ignoring the impulse to remind her—again—that we weren't witches, I looked pointedly at Christopher. "That is thoughtful, setting up a foolproof cover for the use of magic around mundanes."

He curled his lips into a smile, but refused to engage.

That was always the best way to deal with me when I got edgy, so I couldn't fault him.

The shifter glanced back and forth between us. "You'll be there?"

"We will," Christopher said. "But we don't need another sample. We have Paisley."

I kept my mouth shut.

"Okay...I'd better get going." Officer Raymond set down her all-but-untouched tea, plucking a cookie off the plate. "Thank you for the tea." She glanced at me, completely earnest and polite.

So Canadian.

I nodded.

Christopher escorted her to the front door. If she touched him when saying goodbye, there'd be nothing I could do about it. Nothing I should do about it. He was more than capable of moving out of her way if he wanted to.

I nibbled on a ginger snap, lining up all my reasons against helping search for Hannah Stewart in my mind, readying my argument.

Except I was having a difficult time not remembering her smile two days before when I'd gushed over the cardigan she'd set aside for me. Or the way she'd flinched when the bell over the door announced the arrival of her boyfriend. Or how he'd stunk of old beer, as if it was coming out of his pores from the evening before.

Christopher was watching me from the doorway. I couldn't remember all my reasons for not helping. Except that he was mine to protect and Hannah wasn't.

"Paisley and I will go without you," he said. His tone was hard, irreproachable.

As if to punctuate this statement, Paisley ate all the ginger snaps. Including swallowing the plate.

"That's a set," I said mildly.

She gently placed the plate back on the island counter with a flick of her forked blue tongue.

"It would be easier with you," Christopher said. "Quicker."

I picked up my tea, sipping it.

"It will be okay, Socks," he whispered. "I know you're scared —"

"I'm not scared."

He held his hands up but didn't step any farther into the kitchen. "I meant scared for me. For the life you're trying to build for us. But no matter how hard you try to blend in, dressing from the thrift shop, hiring locals to do the work here, or even going to the diner for lunch like a regular person, you know you don't blend in. We don't. Not even to mundane sight. But if we control the attention, we control the gossip. The story. We join the locals looking for Hannah and we find her. Then they'll accept us as one of their own."

"That's not your reasoning."

"No. It's yours."

I swallowed a retort about not being so cold, so calculated. It was better that Christopher didn't know I had other reasons for agreeing to join him. Emotional, irrational reasons. "What's your plan. Using Paisley?"

He nodded. "Starting at Hannah's last known location, which I gathered from Jenni is the diner. Hannah had a shift last night, after working at the thrift store all day."

"Jenni?" I asked mockingly.

Christopher ignored me. "Paisley will pick up Hannah's trail."

"But it's been raining. For weeks." I was being completely snarky, verging on unreasonable. But I loathed being backed into a corner, whether by Christopher or by my own emotions.

"Yes. So … at some point, I'll see you finding the woman."

"Hannah," I corrected softly, gazing at him. "Hannah Stewart." Keying in on me more than he already perpetually did was a terrible idea.

"Let me do this, Socks. I've … I want to stay. I want to plant the garden and paint the barn."

"I know."

"I want to grow flowers and herbs. Dahlias, roses, lavender. I want to cut a few every day and put them on your bedside table."

"I know, Christopher."

"I want to pick the apples and make sauce and pies."

"I know." Tears spiked in my eyes. I struggled to deny them.

"You're tired of running. Tired of dragging me with you. We can make a home here. Let's find Hannah."

"All right."

If we were quick, efficient, the fallout might not be too bad. We were isolated in this small town, so if my immediate future was going to haunt Christopher—more than it already did—we should at least be able to avoid the worst effects.

"You're going to need pants," he said.

"Screw you."

He laughed, turning into the hall. I listened to him jogging upstairs as I reached into the cookie jar for another ginger snap.

Paisley head-butted me in the hip. Hard.

I sighed, then handed her another cookie. She blinked up at me. A single tentacle snaked out from her currently otherwise invisible mane, delicately taking the ginger snap from me. Still pinning me with her red-eyed gaze, her massive maw opened, revealing a double row of sharply pointed teeth. Then she lavishly licked the cookie with her forked tongue.

I laughed.

Then I went upstairs to begrudgingly pull on dark jeans and day hikers. I slipped on a black Gore-Tex jacket. But I wore it over the cashmere cardigan that Hannah Stewart had found for me.

A SMALL GROUP OF PEOPLE WERE GATHERED ON THE corner of South Shore Drive and Lakeview Avenue. Officer Raymond and three others. They fell silent and watchful as Christopher, Paisley, and I arrived at five minutes after three o'clock. On foot, though it was raining lightly. I was assuming the search for Hannah Stewart would take us where I couldn't drive, or wouldn't want to.

The diner on the corner was currently closed but still well lit. The interior was filled with red-vinyl booths arranged next to wide windows. Shiny metal stools topped by the same red vinyl ran along a laminate counter that bisected the restaurant.

A painted sign declared it 'The Home Cafe.'

I'd been meaning to start going to the diner for lunch, once a week, to get the locals accustomed to my presence. But I'd found excuse after excuse to not do so—unpacking, overseeing a few deliveries, rain.

I paused a few feet away from a dark-haired woman who was a couple of inches shorter than me, wearing worn jeans, a bright-green Gore-Tex jacket, and weatherproof hiking boots. I immediately picked up a muted energy from her, informing me that she had latent magic. But what kind, or whether she even knew she was magical, I had no idea.

Her presence was somewhat disconcerting. Before I made the decision to buy the property, I'd been as thorough as possible without actually trespassing onto private property, carefully cataloging and assessing anyone in the area with magic in their blood. I'd visited Lake Cowichan three times, playing the tourist. My magical sensitivity should have been sharp enough to pick up the presence of any Adept. But I'd evidently missed one.

A blond woman in her early forties smiled at us broadly, brushing her hands together as if she thought they might have been dusty. She then thrust one hand in my direction. "Melissa Wilson."

The former daughter-in-law of our neighbors to the west, Melissa had bought the diner with the proceeds of her divorce, going into business with her lover, now husband, but keeping the Wilson surname. And yes, her former mother-in-law had informed me of all that, along with the fact that Melissa had supposedly stolen her tuna casserole recipe, when she'd popped over to introduce herself the day we moved in.

I switched the umbrella to my other hand, shaking Melissa's hand. Her blood didn't hold even a whisper of magic, so I had no reason to refuse the gesture. Her grip was strong. "Emma Johnson."

"You guys bought McGuire Farm last year," she said. "That's nice. It had been empty for far too long. Will you be revitalizing the gardens? The dahlias? We'd love to work out a deal with you on fresh produce. And flowers."

"Melissa." The soft-spoken, balding man at her side smiled. Her second husband, Brian Martin. I'd seen both of their pictures in the local paper. "Let Emma say hello first, at least."

Melissa laughed.

Christopher reached past me, offering his hand to Melissa. "Christopher Johnson."

She took it, shaking his arm enthusiastically while grinning back and forth between us. "Aren't you two something lovely to look at on a cloudy day."

Christopher chuckled. "I was planning on filling the farm stand with any extra produce I manage to grow. And eggs when the chicks come into lay. The dahlias haven't been mulched or lifted to overwinter, so I'm not certain how many will return. But I'm also putting in roses."

Melissa patted the back of his hand. "They'll come back. You're in the perfect spot. Fertile soil, southern exposure." Then she seemed to realize she was still holding on to Christopher, and shook her head slightly as if embarrassed.

But even without touching her to trigger my empathy, I knew she wasn't embarrassed. Human interaction was so terribly odd sometimes.

"This is my husband, Brian. Brian Martin. Together we run the Home Cafe. Jenni says you're going to help look for Hannah. She left here around eight last night. It was a slow evening, and I was happy to pick up any of the tables that arrived in the last hour of the day." She paused to breathe.

Christopher took the opportunity to reach over and shake Brian's hand. Touching mundanes was contact that his magic allowed. Most of the time. Prolonged or long-term contact could trigger a vision, though. But in the moment—while walking in the footsteps of fate, as Christopher would say—he never worried about repercussions, as I did. "Brian."

"Pleased to meet you." Brian hunkered down, offering the back of his hand to Paisley. "And who is this?"

"Paisley."

Christopher and I both paused, waiting to see if the demon dog would behave appropriately, and readying some excuse if she didn't.

Paisley padded forward, wagging her tail, then bumped her head under Brian's open hand. He momentarily lost his balance, but then petted her robustly. "What a beautiful beast you are!"

Paisley chortled, huskily agreeing.

The dark-haired woman in green Gore-Tex thrust her hand toward me. "Lani Zachary, ex-air force technician. I just bought the mechanic shop on MacDonald Road."

I hesitated, staring at her hand and trying to assess the tenor of her magic for a moment too long. Her smile dimmed.

Christopher nudged me with his shoulder, covering the gesture by thrusting his hands in his pockets.

I snagged Lani's hand right before she dropped it. No magic passed between us. "Emma."

"You've got that beautiful 1967 Clearwater Aqua Mustang. I'd love a look at her."

"Oh, sure."

"If you were interested, of course."

I blinked at her, not quite certain what she was asking.

Her smile widened again. "If you were interested in continuing to restore her?"

I nodded. The Mustang was the first truly frivolous thing I'd ever bought myself. I wasn't even remotely a car fanatic. I had just seen it and wanted it. I'd known it would stand out terribly in a small West Coast town where it rained consistently for eight months of the year, but I'd found I couldn't abandon it even after we made the decision to keep moving north of California.

Lani's hand tightened on mine for a brief moment, then she released me.

"We were just waiting for you," Officer Raymond said. "Harry and Tim Morris have the river covered."

"They own Cowichan Kayak and Tubing," Melissa said helpfully.

I nodded, though I'd already known about the Morrises. I had researched every business, every residence I could before we'd even set foot in the town.

Before I'd bought the house and property mostly unseen.

"We're just looking for anyone who has laid eyes on Hannah in the last twenty-four hours." Officer Raymond glanced at everyone in turn. "Try not to panic anyone, eh?"

"What did her mother say, Jenni?" Melissa asked. "She could still be on her way there?"

Officer Raymond nodded. "I called again about fifteen minutes ago. Hannah hasn't checked in. Or answered her text messages or email."

"Hannah's mother is down island in Victoria," Melissa said, speaking to Christopher and me. "She runs a lovely secondhand clothing store on Fort Street."

I also had this information, via Hannah. She'd picked up the cashmere cardigan I was currently wearing under my jacket from her mother's store when she'd gone home the previous weekend. But I nodded anyway.

"Emma and Christopher are going to see if Paisley can pick up any scents from here, and around Hannah's apartment."

"It's been raining pretty steadily," Lani said.

Brian reached over and thumped Paisley on the back. "Are you a good tracker, girl? Have you got a good nose?"

Paisley offered him a toothy smile, fortunately displaying only a single row of teeth. Though it was still possible she was contemplating eating Brian.

I glanced over at Christopher. He nodded shallowly, rubbing the end of Paisley's ear, drawing her attention to him.

"Lani and Melissa will take the main street businesses." Officer Raymond pulled out her cellphone. "You all have my number. I'll be in the cruiser, doing another circuit."

I glanced at Christopher, questioningly this time. He nodded. Again.

Apparently, we did actually have the RCMP officer's number. Christopher had a cellphone. I didn't bother with one. Neither of our magic interacted badly with tech—the Collective had been careful about breeding out any such weaknesses—but I had no need to keep in daily contact with anyone I didn't already live with.

"Brian needs to open the diner," Melissa said. "He'll make sandwiches, so be sure to stop back here when you finish up."

Brian nodded congenially. "And I'll make sure to ask anyone who comes in —"

A gray-haired, red-faced man charged around the corner.

I moved, stepping around Christopher so swiftly that I startled the man. He stopped in his tracks, blinking at me.

Christopher sighed softly, likely shaking his head behind me. But I kept my gaze on the mundane who'd been approaching with such aggression that I could practically feel it boiling off him.

He gaped at me, opening and closing his mouth. I didn't recognize him. My research hadn't always included pictures.

Lani laughed quietly behind me. "Apparently, we've discovered a way to shut Grant up."

"Finally," Jenni Raymond muttered back.

Both of them probably had no idea I could hear them.

"How dare you," so-called Grant howled. "How dare you accuse my boy of malfeasance!"

Officer Raymond thrust herself past me, speaking over her shoulder. "We'll meet back here in an hour unless one of us uncovers a lead."

"I'll have your badge for this!" Grant screeched.

Everyone else ignored him.

"Malfeasance?" Christopher murmured.

I turned my back on the blustering newcomer, whispering, "I'm guessing Grant's his last name. Like Hannah's boyfriend."

Christopher grunted then nodded, agreeing with the connection I'd made.

Based on the huffing and posturing coming from the older Grant, I guessed that Officer Raymond had leveled the same accusation she'd shared with us when she'd knocked on his door a few hours earlier. The accusation she'd used to emotionally blackmail us into helping search for Hannah—that Hannah's boyfriend, Tyler Grant, was physically abusing her.

Christopher kept one eye on the RCMP officer while she attempted to mollify Tyler Grant's father.

I crouched down in front of Paisley, tugging a white tank top out of the front zippered pocket of my jacket. "Don't eat this."

Paisley gummed the edge of the tank top playfully. Then she made a show of sniffing it, like she was attempting to pick up Hannah's scent. It was my tank top, offered up to support the fiction that Paisley was going to be the one who eventually tracked Hannah down.

I wasn't certain what TV shows Paisley had been watching, but I'd never seen a police or tracking dog make such a show of snorting and snuffling, slathering the shirt with slobber while picking up a scent to track.

Christopher laid his hand on my shoulder, slipping his fingers underneath my loose hair and jacket collar. He settled his fingertips along my upper spine, directly over top of the blood tattoo that tied his magic to me.

I was conscious of Lani Zachery's gaze, but I kept my attention on Paisley.

Brian kissed Melissa, then stepped into the diner, flipping the 'Closed' sign hanging in the door to 'Open.'

The older Grant's rant increased in volume behind me, as did Officer Raymond's responses. But I didn't bother following their conversation. We needed to move. Quickly.

"Okay, Paisley," I said, speaking louder than necessary. "Track."

Paisley huffed at me like I was the one overacting. Then she crossed to the door of the diner with her nose hovering over the concrete sidewalk.

I straightened carefully so I didn't knock Christopher's hand away. I met Lani's too-interested gaze, then looked away. Paisley was making a show of picking up Hannah's scent, tapping her paw in various places around the door.

"Let's move?" I asked quietly.

Christopher nodded, dropping his hand. "Let's go find Hannah."

"Paisley appears to have a scent," Lani said, though she'd been more focused on me than on the pit bull.

I nodded, smiling tightly. Then I spoke to Paisley, loudly and clearly. "Show us, girl."

Paisley made a show of snuffling her way back across the sidewalk, where she paused to tap the curb emphatically.

Christopher chuckled under his breath.

"We'll see you back here," Melissa said. "I'll take the north side of South Shore Road, Lani."

The ex-air-force-tech-turned-mechanic nodded in response, though her gaze flicked between me, Christopher, and Paisley. She smiled when she caught my eye.

I turned away, following Paisley across the street between slow-moving cars.

"Witch, I think," Christopher said quietly. "Doesn't know it, though. We're tweaking her instincts."

I nodded. Lani Zachery most definitely knew something was up with us. And when we found Hannah, her suspicions would be confirmed. But what that meant long term, when she didn't even know that she carried latent magic, I had no idea.

Paisley made a show of tracking along the edge of the opposite curb. The thrift store that Hannah ran was only three storefronts to the north.

"You sound like a little piggy," I said, nudging Paisley's backside with my knee.

She looked up at me, snarfling a bit more. Then she dropped the pretense, leading us around the block.

HANNAH'S APARTMENT WAS SITUATED OVER THE thrift store. Both locations were dark, empty of people. Paisley tracked up and down the painted wooden stairs at the back of the gray stucco building. Then she moved out across the small parking lot there. All the spots were empty.

Christopher slipped his cool fingers into the back of my collar, wrapping his hand around the base of my neck. Magic shifted between us without being called or directed. I let it move as it willed. Amplifying Christopher's power without a clear focus could have an adverse effect, casting the magic too far forward in the timeline that stretched endlessly before us.

"Hannah Stewart," I whispered, infusing my words with as much intent as I could muster. "Where are you?"

Paisley crossed back toward us, sitting on her haunches and blinking up at me.

"She left by car?" I asked her.

She pawed the ground.

"Isn't it supposed to be once for yes and twice for no?"

Paisley lost interest in the conversation, wandering off to investigate the garbage bins.

"Hannah Stewart," Christopher murmured.

"Where do you see me, Knox?" I whispered, reverting to his childhood nickname. It was an intimacy I didn't often allow myself. "Where am I about to be?"

Magic welled under Christopher's now-warm palm, sending a hum down my spine. "Ah," he sighed. "Pigs. Farm. Long dirt drive. Outside town. More pigs."

"More pigs," I echoed, rapidly thinking through all the research I'd done into the area.

"Brown house. Two floors. Broken tractor." Christopher dropped his hand from my neck, shoving it into his pocket. "It's raining enough to muddy the edge of the drive. Paisley is leading."

I glanced over at him. The white of his magic ringed his light-gray eyes.

He smiled, blinking the power away. Showing me he was okay, in control.

"Meadow Lane Farm," I said.

"Owned and operated by the Grant family, I presume?"

I nodded grimly. "They used to have a lucrative pig business. There's still remnants of it that come up in internet searches about the area."

"And the farm has withered and died under Grant's not-so-tender care? Since his wife … what? Left him? Or went missing, like Hannah?"

I didn't have an opinion or any verified information to offer, so I focused on the immediate. "We should have brought the car."

"You aren't going to want to leave it behind. We'll be walking at some point. We'll hitch a ride with Jenni."

"No, we won't. Constable Jenni Raymond is useless."

"She'll just slow us down?" he asked mockingly.

I didn't bother answering, turning away from the conversation. "Come on, Paisley. Christopher says you'll pick up Hannah Stewart's scent at a pig farm."

The demon dog cocked her head thoughtfully. Then she stepped into the shadows gathered at the base of the garbage bins and disappeared from sight.

I stared at the empty space. Not even a hint of Paisley's magic remained. Then I glanced over at Christopher, who was holding back laughter.

"I shouldn't have mentioned pigs, right?"

He lost his battle, chortling. "Don't worry, she'll wait for us."

"Before or after she slaughters a pig for dinner and dessert?"

He laughed some more.

"Pigs are sentient beings, you know," I said crossly. "Smarter than dogs and cats."

That amused Christopher even more.

I walked away. Not in a huff, just on a timeline. We were going to need a ride, and I only drove my Mustang.

MEADOW LANE FARM WAS SITUATED ON THE OUT-skirts of Lake Cowichan, actually closer to the nearby village of Youbou than it was to town. Its remoteness might have had something to do with the bylaws of operating a pig farm too close to a body of water or a residential area, but I wasn't certain.

The Mustang chewed up the wet pavement, window wipers rhythmically slapping the steady rain away, and I was pulling through the open gate onto the dirt driveway only fifteen minutes after I'd turned the key in the ignition.

Christopher remained silent as I chose to park on the road side of the barn, rather than drive all the way up to the house. Officer Raymond had already been on the property earlier in the day. And no matter how scent-blind she was, even she couldn't have missed sensing Hannah Stewart if the missing woman was currently in the house.

I stepped out of the car, dropping the keys in the front zippered pocket of my Gore Tex jacket. I tugged the hood over my head but didn't cinch it. It already dampened my hearing too much.

"I suppose protocol would be to text Jenni our location." Christopher stepped around the car, jacket on but not zippered.

"Not our protocol," I said, casting my gaze across the vast expanse of the property. The pens nearest to us were empty, and had been for long enough that grass had grown up around their fence posts. The barn was on the edge of rotting away, in dire need of repair.

"No," Christopher sighed, his tone remote as he lifted his face to the rain. "Not our protocol."

I glanced over, trying to assess his mental state without triggering him further. We hadn't worked together the way we would need to this afternoon since last fall in San Francisco. And even that had been more of a rescue than a dual assignment. That final contract had insured—with the right investments—that I wouldn't have to take another contract for at least a few more years. I hadn't wanted Christopher involved. I'd kept him away from anything I'd had to do with the Adept underworld. It was bad enough that even a subset of magic users knew I existed, without them laying eyes on a clairvoyant of Christopher's power. But I'd been willing to risk too much for the security and stability the money that backed the contract promised.

The sorcerers who'd hired me to amplify a group casting had ensnared me in a blood ward, forcing me to amplify them while slowly draining my magic. They'd bled a young witch in order to hold me at bay, fueling their blood magic with a painfully slow human sacrifice. I might have been able to break free, but doing so would have killed the witch. And as absurd as the thought had seemed in the moment, I found that I couldn't be responsible for the death of an innocent. I couldn't willingly add another stain to my soul.

Christopher had saved me from being murdered—or worse, from another life of slavery. Though he liked to insist that he'd simply been an agent of magic. Him, his sword, and Paisley. But as a result, any Adept who'd managed to walk away from that warehouse and was able to tell the tale knew there were two of us working together. An amplifier and a clairvoyant.

We'd left San Francisco in the early-morning hours without even returning to our rental apartment. We washed off the blood and changed clothing at a highway rest stop a couple of hours later, then slowly made our way north along the coast, across the Canadian border, and into Lake Cowichan. Zig-zagging through small town after small town in the Mustang.

For weeks afterward, I'd been convinced that the Collective was only a step behind us. I was still waiting for them to catch up.

Christopher smiled. "You worry too much, Socks."

"I'm not worrying."

He laughed quietly, blinking at me. The white of his magic clouded his eyes. "Paisley."

I waited a beat, knowing that Christopher was seeing a few minutes ahead. I was out of practice and had missed the transition. That was the reason for his comment about my worrying—what he had seen of my immediate future, not what my present thoughts had been.

The demon dog wandered around the corner. She was slicked with mud, eyes glowing softly red.

"Well," I muttered. "Mud is better than pigs' blood." Or human blood.

Christopher touched my cheek without warning. His fingers were chilly and damp with rain. I flinched.

He blinked away the magic obscuring his sight of the present, frowning at my reaction.

Again, I was out of practice. I scowled at myself. Then I reached over and took his hand.

He nodded.

Paisley ambled away a few steps, then glanced back at me.

"Hannah Stewart," I said, stepping toward the mud-slicked demon dog. "I'm going to find Hannah."

Paisley took off at a fairly steady clip, cutting across the drive toward the empty pens. I followed, tugging Christopher with me.

And for the first time, I genuinely believed that I was going to find the shy, sweet woman who seemed to enjoy setting aside items she thought I'd like at the thrift shop. Even though there was no way she knew me ... not enough to like me.

With Christopher and Paisley with me, there was actually no doubt I'd find Hannah Stewart. And I fervently hoped that she'd be alive when I did.

NO ONE CONFRONTED US AS PAISLEY LED US ALL THE way across the property, pausing at a broken fence post far from the main house. Either the elder Grant was still occupied in town, or he was so drunk he didn't notice trespassers on his land.

That second option wasn't a factually based assessment. Just my instinctual, immediate dislike of the man, and the conclusion that seemed most likely as a result.

I would have preferred a confrontation. Instead, I pushed my hood off my head, glancing back toward the main house, sitting practically on the other side of the property. Then I visually traced a direct line across the wet, muddy ground between the house and where I was standing.

I looked in the opposite direction. Hectares of forest spread out beyond the fence. I hunkered down, peering at a scrap of dark-blue fabric snagged in the crumpled fencing wire only partially attached to the broken fence post.

"Paisley's trail ends here." I spoke out loud unnecessarily, just in case Christopher's magic was listening.

"Which means she's sensed the presence of blood."

I nodded. The rain should have washed any trace amounts away. Unless some had been protected from the elements, possibly in the torn jean fabric attached to the wire fencing. "Why flee for the forest?" I grumbled. "The road was just as close."

"It's harder to run someone down in the woods, Socks." Christopher's tone was kind but remote. His words were laced with magic.

And I was dithering. I knew that my actions, even my unvoiced intentions, would trigger Christopher's next vision of the near future. But I desperately, idiotically, wanted to deny that future at the same time. "Please be alive," I murmured. Then I reached out and plucked the piece of fabric off the fencing wire.

Magic shifted around me, concentrating on the blood tattoo on my spine.

I uncrumpled the fabric. It was smeared with what appeared to be a trace of blood. As expected, but not as I'd hoped.

"Hannah," I whispered, once again purposefully directing, focusing Christopher's power until it prickled along my spine and up my neck. Even without actively amplifying the clairvoyant, we were so tightly bound that a mere decision on my part could alter what he saw of the immediate future. My future. Hannah's future.

He sighed. "You're in the forest. Deep. It's dark. Moving steadily." He lifted his arm, allowing his magic to point the way.

Straight ahead.

Well, I'd known that was coming, hadn't I?

I curled my fingers around the wet fabric, feeling anger welling, warming my chest. By the mess of tracks in the mud between the house and where we stood, Hannah Stewart had fled the house and been chased into the woods. She'd ripped her jeans, scratching herself deeply enough to bleed, when she'd tried to climb over this section of fencing. I glanced at the post, the break looked new. Then, sometime later, Tyler Grant had been seen racing away from town.

Constable Jenni Raymond was ridiculously useless. A shapeshifter should have been able to find Hannah hours ago, despite the rain.

I took a couple of steps away from the fence. Christopher followed. I bent down, tightening the laces on my boots until they were almost uncomfortable.

Christopher did the same, his magic completely obscuring his eyes.

"If she's dead," I said, speaking to that magic even as I made the request to the clairvoyant, "I'll need you to lead me to Taylor Grant."

A smile flitted across his face. "And what will you do to him, Emma?"

I settled my gaze on the thick swath of trees beyond the fence. "I'll chase him through the forest until he dies of terror. Then I'll feed him to his father's pigs."

I sprang forward. Touching down with my right foot, I leaped the fence. Paisley appeared at my side as I landed, having jumped almost at the same time as me. My feet shifted in the muddy wild grass, but my ankles didn't twist.

Christopher landed next to me. His magic brushed against the side of my face, keeping tabs on me.

With Paisley slightly to my side and Christopher tight at my back, I jogged steadily toward the trees. Then I was within their depths, swallowed by evergreens that had stood for hundreds of years.

One tree had fallen over another, creating a high barrier in front of us. A blockage that would be best skirted.

But Hannah had fled in terror. She would have gone—

"Over," Christopher murmured.

Spotting two footholds, I leaped the barrier, landing in a bed of moss and dried needles on the other side. The rain barely penetrated the thick evergreen boughs overhead.

Paisley leaped over me, landing two paces beyond the trees. She looked back at me with glowing red eyes, snorting her impatience.

Slightly slower, Christopher followed.

"Straight?" I asked.

He nodded.

I took off after Paisley, picking up my pace and darting around any obstacle that I doubted Hannah could have easily climbed. Keeping to the path she'd most likely taken, as best as I could guess.

After about fifty paces, Christopher spoke. "Left. Three trees. Right. Five. Then … " He trailed off.

I darted left, counting three fir trees. Then I cut right, counting five more fir trees and instantly spotted what Christopher hadn't articulated.

A small clearing held the remains of a building and evidence that someone had camped there recently, or at least built a fire with a ring of rocks. The building was decrepit. Rotting wood siding, no glass in the windows or door in the open frame.

I had no ability to process evidence and estimate any sort of timeline, but I knew what the signs of a struggle looked like. Some sort of fight had taken place in the clearing, scuffing the dirt and moss, trampling the ferns around the edges.

I darted forward, investigating the decrepit structure. It was empty of people. Or bodies. Thankfully. Various names and initials had been carved or burned into the wood frame of the door over many years. Melted candles collected rain in the windows. Empty beer cans were scattered around dark corners. I didn't bother peering into the dark any longer than was necessary to determine that Hannah wasn't trapped or tied up within its depths. I wasn't certain what the building's function had originally been, but it wasn't any sort of shelter now.

I stepped back into the clearing.

Christopher was standing by the makeshift firepit, gazing out at the forest. "Something bad happened here," he whispered. "Can you feel it?"

"Magic? Or with Hannah?"

Christopher shook his head. "Not Hannah. But I feel exceedingly blessed that I wasn't given the ability to see the past when my genes were magically spliced in a test tube on level five."

I waited to see if he would elaborate further, shoving the echo of our shared past—destroying the compound within which we were created—from my mind as quickly as it had surfaced.

Christopher didn't elaborate, though.

"He caught up to her here," I said, gesturing at the scuff marks all around us.

"Very likely."

"Why stop?"

"She's hurt." Christopher stepped to the side, indicating a smaller set of footprints. Every second one was preceded and followed by short drag marks. "Limping."

Paisley snarled quietly, calling my attention to a rock that looked as though it had rolled to the edge of the clearing.

"Blood?" I asked Paisley.

She tapped the ground once.

Though we'd been teasing earlier, that apparently meant 'yes' now.

"Can you track it?"

She tilted her head, then glanced back in the direction we'd just come—toward the property and the house.

That didn't make any sense. Unless...

"It isn't Hannah's blood?"

Paisley lay down and started grooming her left foot.

"She got a piece of Tyler." I laughed huskily. "Then she continued to run. He gave up the chase."

"Or she knocked him out of it."

"Where did she exit the clearing?"

Christopher brushed his fingers against my cheek, his magic flooding his eyes. "Where does Socks exit the clearing?" he murmured.

He pointed to our left, past the decrepit structure. Then he pressed a small flashlight into my hand. I turned without another word, stepping back into the forest.

AFTER THIRTY OR FORTY MORE MINUTES OF BEING directed by the occasional soft murmur from Christopher, I spotted evidence that someone had crawled through the underbrush. Paisley led me along that trail for another ten minutes before I found Hannah Stewart.

I swept my flashlight across her, not completely certain she was actually still alive. She was curled up in the shelter of a fallen tree, huddled under a lined plaid jacket that was too large for her.

A fierce pride rippled through me. She'd taken Tyler down, then stolen his jacket.

"Hannah," I whispered, not wanting to spook her. The day had already been gray, but now that the sun was near setting, the forest was encased in a deep gloom. "Hannah?"

She didn't answer.

Paisley padded out of the darkness, brushing against my leg. I stepped forward with Christopher beside me. Hunkering down, I brushed my hand over Hannah's shoulder.

She mewed softly in her sleep.

I exhaled in relief, rotating the flashlight in my hand so it pointed upward, illuminating us. I didn't want to blind her. Then I touched her shoulder again.

Hannah opened her eyes, blinking up at me. But it was Christopher hovering over my shoulder who she saw first. Pure awe spread across her scraped and bruised face. "Oh ... " she sighed. "Am I dead then?"

Christopher chuckled.

"Not yet," I said.

Hannah's gaze flicked to me, then back at Christopher. "But ... but ... you ... you aren't angels?" She got her arm untangled from the jacket, reaching a shaking hand toward me. Then recognition dawned across her face. "Emma?"

"Yes."

Her eyes darted over to Christopher. "I thought … I thought … you were glowing."

Christopher stepped away, just in case she was picking up the magic that had taken up permanent residence in his eyes.

"It's just the flashlight," I said, covering. "Can you walk?"

Hannah's face crumpled. She shook her head, then gasped in pain. She'd been beaten. Badly. "My ankle is broken, or sprained, I think. And my arm … I guess I shouldn't have kept running."

"You always keep running, Hannah. Always. You make whoever is after you kill you in order to take you down."

She looked up at me, her eyes filling with tears.

"You were magnificent," I said. "You were brave and fierce, Hannah Stewart."

Her chin trembled. "I waited too long … too long to say no."

"You're here, aren't you? You made it."

"Yeah … " Her voice firmed. "Yeah, I made it."

"I'm going to carry you."

"You … " She glanced toward Christopher. "You're going to carry me?"

"Yeah. We'll trade off if necessary." I passed the flashlight to Christopher, then took Hannah's arm, placing it over my shoulder. "I'm sorry. Every step is going to hurt."

"It's okay. I can handle the pain."

I gathered her legs, then straightened with her cradled in my arms. She moaned, stifling her reaction.

"You're so strong," she murmured.

"Yes," I said. "Maybe don't mention it to anyone?"

She laughed quietly. "As long as you don't tell anyone that I thought you were angels."

"Deal."

IT WAS FULLY DARK, BUT THE RAIN HAD STOPPED BY the time Paisley led us to a logging road. From there, we headed back toward Meadow Lane Farm. Even with Hannah possibly traumatized, I wasn't leaving the Mustang any longer than I needed to.

Finding he had a weak cellular signal, Christopher texted Officer Raymond.

About ten minutes later, he wordlessly turned back to me, reaching for and settling Hannah between us with one of her arms over each of our shoulders. It was a much more painful hold for her, but it wouldn't make it obvious that I was capable of carrying a fifty-five-kilo woman over uneven ground for so long.

There was nothing we could do about Christopher's eyes. They still glowed. And the way Hannah kept darting awestruck glances his way might have indicated that she could see the manifestation of his magic. It also might have meant that she was simply enamored by the first person she'd set eyes on after imagining her own death.

She didn't have to articulate that. I knew. There was no way she'd dragged herself through that forest only to collapse exhausted without imagining she was slipping toward death.

It wasn't my first time rescuing someone. Just as I, too, had been rescued on the brink of that abyss.

The flashing lights of an RCMP cruiser appeared on the road ahead.

We stepped off to the side, waiting for Officer Raymond to catch us with her headlights.

The cruiser screeched to a halt. The flashing lights hurt my eyes, too bright after walking in the dark for almost an hour. Officer Raymond barreled out of the vehicle, leaving the door open as she ran toward us.

"Thank you, Emma," Hannah whispered. "Christopher. Thank you. And Paisley."

Then the shapeshifter practically tore the injured woman out of our arms. "You are pressing charges," she growled at Hannah, hauling her toward the cruiser without a glance our way. "This time you are pressing charges."

Hannah didn't answer, most likely because being moved so roughly was a painful process. I tamped my mouth shut. It wasn't my place to admonish an officer of the law.

Christopher smirked at me.

Officer Raymond got Hannah situated in the front passenger seat, where she laid her head back wearily. Though her gaze still rested on Christopher. He must have appeared otherworldly illuminated by the headlights, despite having his hands stuffed in the pockets of a perfectly ordinary navy-blue Gore-Tex jacket.

The shifter shut Hannah's door, jogging back around the cruiser. "What are you waiting for?" she barked at us. "Get in. I'll drop you on the way to the hospital."

When neither of us answered or stepped forward compliantly, she finally looked at us. She flinched. "Jesus."

So that answered the question about Christopher's eyes. He bowed his head and started walking. I followed. Though still mostly overcast, the evening was just bright enough to mark the edges of the road. Paisley skulked alongside in the dark ditch.

"Wait," the shifter called. "I need a statement. How you found her … I mean, how you used the dog to find her, and —"

"Hannah knows where to find us," I said over my shoulder. "If she wants to press charges."

"That is unacceptable. You are in my —"

I spun back, leveling a look her way. "You asked for our help, Jenni Raymond, without imposing conditions. You'll take what we give. We are bound to do no more than that."

"I'll take what you give? Or what?"

I smiled.

Christopher laughed from somewhere in the dark behind me.

Doubt flickered over the shifter's face.

I cast my voice low, though I was fairly certain Hannah was probably already asleep. "Use your nose, shifter."

Her nostrils flared. Then she glared, as if angered that she'd obeyed my command. And yes, that alone should have reminded her who was the alpha in our relationship.

Me.

"Smell the magic now?" I asked mockingly.

Then I turned away without waiting for an answer. I had my Mustang to collect, hopefully before Christopher crashed.

CHRISTOPHER DIDN'T LEAVE HIS BEDROOM FOR TWO days, keeping a locked door between us. On the third day, he made it downstairs, fed himself a bowl of cereal, then didn't move from the couch except to use the facilities.

I went as far as to turn on the TV, queue up Netflix, and give him the remote. But he didn't watch anything, except for the glimpses of the future playing out in his mind's eye.

My future. Christopher's magic simmered, spiking every time I drew near. He suffered in silence, but I could actually feel his energy tracking me around the house, far more intensely than it usually did.

It rained. The house was cold. I cranked the heat because Christopher was the only one who knew how to make a fire without smoking us out.

I brought him tea and ginger snaps. I tried to coerce him into the barn by shooting short videos of the chicks that I played back on the TV. I'd had to figure out how to take care of the three-week-old chickens myself, carefully filling in the daily log that Christopher had started in a wire-bound notebook.

Keeping ourselves perpetually organized was one of the ways we'd learned to combat all the darkness that continually threatened to take up residence in our minds. In our souls. Not that we discussed it. I made an effort to not even acknowledge it. Because it wasn't something I could fix or solve.

On the fourth day, I took Christopher's phone from his room, charging it so I could have the option of scrolling through his address book. Then I layered up, went outside, and sat in the Mustang parked in the barn. Paisley joined me. Though I knew she would have preferred to watch over the chicks, I didn't tell her to leave.

I had never missed the balance of having the other three around quite so acutely as I did that fourth day. If the rest of the Five had been with us, Christopher's magic wouldn't have been so tightly tied to me.

I had long suspected that he had phone numbers or email addresses for the other three. I knew that he had maintained at least some level of contact with Bee.

"Amanda," I murmured, gazing down at the phone and correcting myself, using the name on her passport rather than the nickname Christopher had given her before he'd even had a name himself.

Because when we were young, her magic had felt like bumblebees in his head.

I paused, hoping, breathing, believing that the telepath would hear me. That somehow, no matter how many hundreds or thousands of kilometers separated us, she'd feel my need through our blood tattoo connection.

Christopher wouldn't have been on the couch and I wouldn't have been stuck in the chilly car if the other three were with us. Even if it was just Bee who was with us.

If we'd been the Five, we would have found Hannah in minutes, not hours.

Actually, no.

We wouldn't have looked at all.

Hannah might have died, of exposure or starvation. And I wouldn't have cared.

The person I used to be wouldn't have cared. Because I wouldn't have taken the chance, or even have had the chance to know Hannah at all.

I wanted to care. I was glad—happy, even—that we'd gone out into the rain, hiked through the forest, and come out with Hannah.

Then we'd come home. Christopher, Paisley, and me. I had parked the Mustang in the barn and we'd climbed into our beds.

Under our roof. Our house. Our place in the world.

And that was worth much more than a few moments, or even days, of discomfort.

Bee didn't magically reach out.

I set the phone aside, its address book unexplored. I crushed my insecurities. I could take care of Christopher for however long it was going to take for him to become more than simply a conduit for his magic.

I got out of the car and went back inside.

Christopher was watching an action movie. Something set in space with a talking raccoon. It looked good, fun. Funny.

I went into the kitchen, wrestled dinner out of a can of tomato soup and the toaster, then settled on the opposite side of the couch. Christopher nibbled on his liberally buttered toast and restarted the movie.

His magic reached out and caressed my cheek. I ignored it and it left me alone.

PERCHED ON THE EDGE OF THE RED-VINYL BOOTH, I gazed at the piping-hot tuna casserole Melissa Wilson had just set before me, identifying mushrooms, peas, and what appeared to be leeks among the cream-coated penne noodles.

Melissa laughed. "You bite it, dear. Not the other way around."

The owner and operator of the Home Cafe was in no way old enough to be calling me 'dear.' But she was trying to be friendly, so I didn't complain.

"It smells good," I murmured, spreading my paper napkin across my lap and picking up my fork.

"Fresh-grated parmesan," Melissa said, rather jovially for someone discussing a baked cheese topping.

The front door of the diner opened. Lani Zachery entered, smiling as she cast her gaze across the counter, then over the full booths.

I turned my attention back to the steaming pile of food in front of me, so that I didn't appear to be staring at her. I'd selected the farthest booth in the far corner of the diner. The window to my right, the wall at my back. If attacked directly, I'd have more than enough warning. Enough to exit the booth and vault the counter, if not time enough to confront the assault head-on. If someone or something tried to come through the window, I could roll away before it had even cracked.

And yes, I recognized that those were odd thoughts to be having over lunch at the local diner in a town of three thousand people—none of whom were powerful enough to even scratch me.

Lani settled her gaze on me, then started walking my way. I could actually feel the tiny shift in her latent magic as she did so. Witch power, Christopher had classified it. Lani paused, murmuring greetings to a few locals who had eyed me when I arrived. But Melissa had greeted me by name exuberantly, and the other customers' wariness had eased.

An article from the local newspaper was clipped out and pinned to the bulletin board by the door. It detailed the rescue of a local woman by new residents, Emma and Christopher Johnson, and their dog, Paisley. According to the article, Hannah Stewart had gone hiking and gotten lost in the woods.

Hannah hadn't pressed charges. Not yet, at least. At least not in any way that was public knowledge. And even if it wasn't any of my business, the idea that Tyler was going to walk away from it all bothered me, quietly festering in the back of my mind.

The day after the article had been printed and posted online, casseroles and baking had started appearing in the broken-down farm stand at the end of our drive, which I kept gated always. I was fairly certain that it was Melissa's banana bread that finally got Christopher off the couch and back into turning over and mulching the garden.

"Emma," Lani said, pausing beside my booth.

I looked up, offering her a smile. "Lani."

"I was thinking we should set a date."

"A date?" I echoed.

"For you to bring by the Mustang." She grinned at me. "Unless you want me to just drop in."

The offer to just drop in sounded loaded. But with what, I wasn't certain. "Actually, the car is due for a tune-up."

"Perfect. Tuesday? Drop her at the shop by 9:00 A.M."

"I will."

She hesitated, a lick of magic coiling around her as she eyed me. Then she laughed quietly. "Don't worry, I won't ask to join you."

Her magic was intriguing. Manifesting as intuition, perhaps. Though I wasn't certain how that would tie into the air force or the mechanic side of her life, so perhaps it was more than that.

I smiled. "Another time."

Her grin widened as she stepped back to the counter, her gaze sweeping over me. "Count on it."

Then she sat down, turning her back on me and ordering a turkey burger with Havarti.

I nibbled at the tuna casserole—ordered because Melissa had recommended it and I'd never eaten anything like it—and found it exceedingly tasty.

ON MY WAY BACK TO THE HOUSE, I NOTICED THAT someone—or multiple people, perhaps—had come by and fixed up the farm stand at the top of the drive. It was now painted white with a red metal roof, matching the main house. A sign had been attached to it, seemingly declaring the property to be White Owl Farm.

My breath caught in my throat, and some sort of emotion seized my chest. For a moment, I thought I was suffocating. Then I realized I was overwhelmed.

With … joy.

I forced myself to breathe. In and out. Steady, steady. Then I reached up and touched the carving of the owl on one side of the lettering—a white owl. Possibly a reference to the color of Christopher's hair? Possibly because we'd found Hannah Stewart in the forest at night?

In the aftermath of that night, I had waited for three days after the newspaper article came out, my blades near to hand though I didn't open their wooden case. I'd waited for someone to come for us, even though we hadn't been pictured, just named.

But no one came. And Christopher had been right about stepping up when we'd been asked. About being accepted by the community in which we wanted to make a home.

Paisley appeared at my side, gently relieving me of the second order of tuna casserole Melissa had insisted I bring back for Christopher, 'since everyone knows he's a slave to the garden right now.'

Even cloistered on our property, the community saw us. And accepted us.

Paisley slipped through the gate, leading the way back to the house.

I paused at the mailbox, retrieving a package I'd been waiting for. I'd intended it to be a birthday gift for Christopher in August, but he needed it now.

I WAS LAYING OUT TEA WHEN CHRISTOPHER ENTERED the kitchen through the French-paned doors. He left his jacket slung over the railing, having removed his gloves and washed his hands and feet in the barn sink that he'd just replaced. The old one had been leaking.

We both ignored the way his magic spiked when it keyed in on me. It ebbed as quickly as it had swelled.

"Tea?" he asked absentmindedly. His gaze fell on the small rectangular package on the island. It was wrapped in brown paper and addressed to him. "A gift?"

"Yes." I set the kettle on the stove and lit the gas burner.

Christopher picked up the package, carefully peeling the paper open and enjoying the ritual of doing so. Even after seven years, gifts were still a novelty. Owning anything at all was still something to celebrate.

Christopher freed a plain white box from its wrappings, opening it to reveal a set of cards. He carefully allowed them to fall out into his open palm, gasping as he closed his hand over them.

Witch magic.

I couldn't feel it myself. My senses tuned into people more than magical things, unless the artifact or casting was particularly powerful. But I'd had the cards designed and inked by a witch, so I knew what Christopher felt when he held them.

He plucked the top card from the pack, flipping it over to reveal a black-inked botanical drawing of a sunflower. The word 'Freedom' had been hand-lettered below the image.

"Oracle cards," I said, continuing to set out mugs, napkins, and ginger snaps to accompany our tea. Then I carefully measured out the perfect amount of Quanzhou milk oolong into the strainer, setting it into the previously warmed teapot. Keeping myself occupied instead of watching Christopher too closely. He didn't need to feel extra pressure from me.

"Crafted by a witch," he said. His voice was hushed, almost a whisper.

"Yes. A witch skilled in herbology. I commissioned the cards just after we arrived here. I was going to build you an entire set for your birthday. This is just the first twenty-two. So you can add to the deck later."

He reverently flipped over cards that were labeled Manifestation, Wisdom, Development, and Security. "It follows the basic tarot suits. But it's been adapted to include corresponding plants, and tied to individual intention?"

"Yes."

He grinned at me. Then he shuffled the deck three different times, three different ways. His magic struck, encompassing the cards in his hands and flooding through his eyes. Then the power settled into its regular hum.

He laughed, delighted.

The kettle whistled. Which gave me an excuse to turn my back for the moment it took to retrieve it and turn off the gas. Time to hide my relief that Christopher's clairvoyance had accepted the cards, claimed them.

I poured the hot water through the strainer in the teapot, setting the timer so it would steep for exactly five minutes, as I preferred for the milk oolong.

Christopher shuffled the cards for a long while. Then finally, he drew three, placing them side by side next to the plate of ginger snaps.

The cards came up Ginger, Strawberry, Rose.

Manifestation. Movement. Partnership.

Humming in the back of his throat, he collected the cards, shuffled, then drew from the top again.

Ginger. Strawberry. Rose.

He stared at the cards for a moment. Then he looked up at me.

"What does it mean?" I said.

"Well, ginger is obviously you."

I glanced at the card titled Manifestation. "How so?"

"Action. Awareness. Concentration ... a boost of power. That's you." He scooped up the cards and reshuffled, drawing again.

Ginger. Strawberry. Rose.

Manifestation. Movement. Partnership.

Christopher threw back his head and laughed. "Three times. Well, I'd say that's pretty set in stone."

The timer went off. I pulled the strainer out of the tea, setting it aside. Then I turned off the timer.

Christopher was still grinning at me. "Don't worry, Fox in Socks. It will be a short fall and a soft landing. I'm looking forward to it immensely." Chuckling to himself, he scooped up the cards, tucked them back in the box, then slipped them into his back pocket. He poured the tea.

I had no idea what he was talking about. Except I was fairly certain—based on my conversations with the witch I'd commissioned the cards from—that rose most often stood for love, usually romantic. And strawberry? Paired with the rose and the ginger ... it could stand for victory or luck or ... pleasure.

Christopher eyed me over the top of his tea mug, silently goading me to ask for clarification.

"*Downton Abbey*?" I asked archly, picking up and placing the ginger snaps, the teapot, and my mug onto a tray. Then I exited through the dining room, crossing into the front sitting room without begging to know what he'd just glimpsed of my future.

I was more than happy to take each step believing that it came with some freedom of choice. I'd deal with whatever—or whoever—the strawberry and rose cards represented when it was time to do so, not fret about it beforehand.

APRIL 2018.

For two months, I had weighed the thought of hunting down Tyler Grant.

I had mulled over how I might track a mundane that Jenni Raymond was undoubtedly already on the hunt for via all the nonmagical channels available to her. Credit card activity and all that. Instead, I'd settled on getting Christopher's help to set up basic perimeter warning spells at Hannah's apartment and thrift shop. We'd contained the spells to the exterior doorways, worried that anything else would be too complicated for us to cast with any success. Christopher had more of an ability with witch magic than I did, so he'd done the actual casting. I was perfectly suited to be the one to extricate the hair sample needed from the Grants' house without Tyler's father even knowing I was on the property.

I had doubts that the spell would work. Tyler wasn't magical in the least. But though it was still really none of my business, the entire episode had felt unfinished. Raw. Exposed.

Hannah still hadn't pressed charges.

Tyler Grant tripped one of the perimeter spells just after two in the morning. I found him pressed up against Hannah's exterior apartment door fifteen minutes later. He was still in the begging stage of trying to talk her into opening the door, though as I slowly climbed the painted wood exterior stairs, I had no doubt he'd start pounding on it soon enough.

His timing couldn't have been better. Hannah wasn't home and the night was dark. Cloudy, raining.

Paisley, wearing her regular pit bull form, prowled alongside me until we stepped silently onto the well-lit top landing. Then she wandered off along the shadowed exterior walkway to our left, likely casing the neighboring apartments. Or she was looking for cats. Christopher had decided the demon dog wanted a pet, and that coincidentally, we needed a barn cat. I hadn't given in to either of them yet.

Tyler was completely oblivious to my presence, cooing something incoherent to the doorjamb.

I could kill him.

Snap his neck.

He'd never see me coming. He'd never even hear death stalking him.

But catching a hint of the stale beer and unwashed stench with which he was polluting the fresh night air, I realized I preferred to extract a lingering, more gut-wrenching retribution. Even though I had no right to such retribution myself.

Good thing I was comfortable operating in absentia.

So Hannah Stewart would never have to face her abuser again. No matter how capable she was of doing so, it would still hurt her.

"Hannah's not here," I said, pausing a few steps away.

Tyler Grant flinched, spinning around and sloshing some of the beer in the open can he held onto his torn jeans and light-brown work boots. Boots that didn't appear to have ever seen a day of work on an actual job site. Three other cans of beer were still held in a six-pack plastic holder, set on the floor next to the door.

He eyed me. I was the same height as him, wearing an oversized wool sweater over a dress and sneakers, with my hair pulled back into a low ponytail.

"Who are you?" he slurred. "New neighbor?"

"Something like that."

"Where is she, then?"

I didn't answer, even though I knew Hannah was visiting her mother for the weekend. She'd mentioned it at the diner two days before.

"I ain't disturbing you."

"You do disturb me. But there's an easy fix."

He frowned, blinking at me and swaying slightly on his feet. Then he purposefully straightened, raking a heated gaze over me. His lips curled disdainfully. He was wearing a school jacket from a university I would have bet he'd either never attended or had failed out of in his first year.

A lusty grin slowly stretched across Tyler's face. There was something nasty in the expression.

Good.

"What's your name, sweetheart?" he asked, puffing up his chest and swaying slightly.

"I've been waiting for you," I said, closing the space between us until he was within easy reach.

He blinked at me again. Then he grinned. "Really? You want some Tyler, eh babe?"

"Something like that, yes."

He nodded. "I've got beer if you've got a bed nearby."

I grinned. "How do you know Hannah hasn't pressed charges? Did your daddy tell you it was okay to come back into town?"

He stopped smiling. "What do you know about it, bitch?"

I took a step closer, our noses practically touching. "I know that you deserve to take everything you ever did to Hannah Stewart. Every slap, every punch, and more."

"Yeah?" he jeered. "And who's going to deliver it?"

"Me."

He snorted.

Paisley, still appearing to be a regular pit bull, stepped out of the darkness right beside me, mumbling discontentedly. Probably because I hadn't waited to include her in the threatening part of the proceedings.

Tyler flinched, stumbling back until he was pressed against Hannah's door.

I sighed.

"You crazy bitch," he snarled, his gaze flicking between the pit bull and me. "You can't just walk up and threaten someone like that."

"No? What if our genders were reversed? Then would it be okay for me to threaten you? To beat you up? Chase you into the forest?"

He straightened, fighting through his inebriation for some bravado. "You know what? Maybe it's you who needs to be put in your place."

I smiled. "Are you the man to do it, Tyler?"

"Hell yeah, I am."

He stepped forward.

I let him grab me.

He wrapped his hands around my upper arms, trying to yank me off my feet. He didn't even manage to move me.

"You're stretching my sweater. I like this sweater."

"What the fuck?" he muttered. Then he stepped back and swung for me, openhanded.

I grabbed his arm midstrike. Then, quite deliberately—so he could see me do it—I snapped his wrist.

He howled in pain, hunching over. His open can of beer hit the landing, fizzing all over.

Paisley knocked him all the way down with a lazy swipe. He keeled over, then scrambled back to press himself against the door again, hunched over and holding his arm.

I glanced around. No lights flicked on in any of the nearby apartments or houses behind us. I stepped closer, leaning over Tyler. "Care to try again?"

He kicked out.

I broke his ankle.

He shrieked.

Paisley chortled.

I straightened to survey the neighborhood again. Still quiet. Though honestly, I had no doubt that even if the neighbors were inclined to report a disturbance, the local law would back any version of any story I related to them.

Tyler broke down into mewling sobs.

"Really?" I asked. "That's all it takes to make you cry?"

"You're crazy," he muttered wetly. "I could call the cops."

"And I could have just killed you." I crouched beside the sniveling coward, grabbing his face and twisting his head to force eye contact. "Couldn't I, Tyler? I could kill you right now. Then I'd pack you into the trunk of your own car, drive you home, and feed you to your father's pigs."

He sniveled, wiping his nose with his uninjured hand. "Why don't you then, bitch?"

"Because I'm not that sort of person anymore. Or…to be completely accurate, I don't want to be that person anymore. Unless I'm pushed. Do you want to push me, Tyler?"

He shook his head sharply.

"I can't hear you. Do you want to push me?"

"No."

"So what are you going to do about it?"

"Leave Hannah alone."

"Hmm. Actually that doesn't seem good enough, does it? So how about this. If you ever raise your hand to another woman ever again, I'll know it."

"That's not possible. What are you going to do? Devote your life to tailing me?"

I grinned at him.

He flinched.

"I just might. You'll never know, will you? And if it isn't me, you'd better believe that someone will be around to beat your ass." I reached forward so quickly that he wouldn't have seen me move. Then I paused.

Watching the terror dawn on his face, I flicked his nose.

He peed his pants.

Well, that was disgusting. And honestly, he'd folded a little too quickly to fully satisfy my desire for vengeance.

I sighed, straightening to pull Christopher's cellphone out of my pocket. Then I texted Tyler's location to Jenni Raymond as I wandered down the dark exterior stairs and into the back parking lot. I eyed his car while I waited for a reply.

"Hey, Paisley," I murmured. "You want to puncture some tires?"

Chortling quietly to herself, the demon dog slunk around the car, systematically shredding each tire.

The cellphone pinged.

>*I'll be right there.*

He isn't going anywhere quickly.

I tucked the phone in my pocket and wandered back toward the Mustang. I could have given the RCMP officer a heads-up the moment Tyler triggered the perimeter spell. I could have—I should have—stayed out of it. But there had just been too many other times that I'd been forced to walk away. Too many people who'd died because I couldn't or wouldn't save them.

Hannah Stewart wasn't going to end up on that list.

I wasn't certain Jenni could persuade Hannah to press charges. But now the RCMP officer's efforts would be backed by mine. By me.

I drove home, ignoring the series of text messages that pinged through on Christopher's cellphone as Jenni Raymond peppered me with questions. Unless Tyler told her differently, the RCMP officer would think Christopher had broken his wrist and ankle. And Tyler Grant was never going to admit that a woman beat him.

That was fine by me. On both counts.

The house was dark when I arrived home. I climbed back into bed, burrowed under the quilt, and fell asleep contentedly.

Acknowledgements

With thanks to:

MY STORY & LINE EDITOR
Scott Fitzgerald Gray

MY PROOFREADER
Pauline Nolet

MY BETA READERS
Didi Brady, Michelle Burdan, Karen Hunt Colvin,
Anteia Consorto, Terry Daigle, Angela Flannery,
Gael Fleming, Stacey Mackes, Beth Patterson,
Megan Gayeski Pirajno, and Heather Pesaresi.

**FOR THEIR CONTINUAL ENCOURAGEMENT,
FEEDBACK, & GENERAL ADVICE**
SFWA
The Office
The Retreat

About the Author

MEGHAN CIANA DOIDGE IS AN AWARD-WINNING WRITER based out of Salt Spring Island, British Columbia, Canada. She has a penchant for bloody love stories, superheroes, and the supernatural. She also has a thing for chocolate, potatoes, and cashmere.

For recipes, giveaways, news, and glimpses of upcoming stories, please connect with Meghan on her:

New release mailing list, http://eepurl.com/AfFzz
Personal blog, www.madebymeghan.ca
Twitter, @mcdoidge
Facebook, Meghan Ciana Doidge
Email, info@madebymeghan.ca

Please also consider leaving an honest review at your point of sale outlet.

ALSO BY MEGHAN CIANA DOIDGE

NOVELS
After the Virus
Spirit Binder
Time Walker
Cupcakes, Trinkets, and Other Deadly Magic (Dowser 1)
Trinkets, Treasures, and Other Bloody Magic (Dowser 2)
Treasures, Demons, and Other Black Magic (Dowser 3)
I See Me (Oracle 1)
Shadows, Maps, and Other Ancient Magic (Dowser 4)
Maps, Artifacts, and Other Arcane Magic (Dowser 5)
I See You (Oracle 2)
Artifacts, Dragons, and Other Lethal Magic (Dowser 6)
I See Us (Oracle 3)
Catching Echoes (Reconstructionist 1)
Tangled Echoes (Reconstructionist 2)
Unleashing Echoes (Reconstructionist 3)
Champagne, Misfits, and Other Shady Magic (Dowser 7)
Misfits, Gemstones, and Other Shattered Magic (Dowser 8)
Gemstones, Elves, and Other Insidious Magic (Dowser 9)
Demons and DNA (Amplifier 1)

NOVELLAS/SHORTS
Love Lies Bleeding
The Graveyard Kiss (Reconstructionist 0.5)
Dawn Bytes (Reconstructionist 1.5)
An Uncut Key (Reconstructionist 2.5)
Graveyards, Visions, and Other Things that Byte (Dowser 8.5)
The Amplifier Protocol (Amplifier 0)
Close to Home (Amplifier 0.5)

Please also consider leaving an honest
review at your point of sale outlet.

DOWSER SERIES ✦ BOOK 1

CUPCAKES, TRINKETS, *and other* DEADLY MAGIC

MEGHAN CIANA DOIDGE

DOWSER SERIES ✦ BOOK 2

TRINKETS, TREASURES, *and other* BLOODY MAGIC

MEGHAN CIANA DOIDGE

DOWSER SERIES ✦ BOOK 3

TREASURES, DEMONS, *and other* BLACK MAGIC

MEGHAN CIANA DOIDGE

DOWSER SERIES ✦ BOOK 4

SHADOWS, MAPS, *and other* ANCIENT MAGIC

MEGHAN CIANA DOIDGE

DOWSER SERIES ✦ BOOK 5

MAPS, ARTIFACTS, *and other* ARCANE MAGIC

MEGHAN CIANA DOIDGE

DOWSER SERIES ✦ BOOK 6

ARTIFACTS, DRAGONS, *and other* LETHAL MAGIC

MEGHAN CIANA DOIDGE

ORACLE SERIES ✦ BOOK 1

I SEE ME

MEGHAN CIANA DOIDGE

ORACLE SERIES ✦ BOOK 2

I SEE YOU

MEGHAN CIANA DOIDGE

ORACLE SERIES ✦ BOOK 3

I SEE US

MEGHAN CIANA DOIDGE

RECONSTRUCTIONIST SERIES ✦ BOOK 1

Catching Echoes

MEGHAN CIANA DOIDGE

RECONSTRUCTIONIST SERIES ✦ BOOK 2

Tangled Echoes

MEGHAN CIANA DOIDGE

RECONSTRUCTIONIST SERIES ✦ BOOK 3

Unleashing Echoes

MEGHAN CIANA DOIDGE

Made in the USA
Columbia, SC
26 June 2025

59862303R00159